MARGOT AND MATEO SAVE THE WORLD

Also by Darcy Miller
Roll

MARGOT AND MATEO SAVE THE WORLD

WITHDRAWN

DARCY MILLER

HARPER
An Imprint of HarperCollinsPublishers

Library of Congress Control Number: 2017944388

ISBN 978-0-06-246131-5

Typography by Katie Klimowicz

18 19 20 21 22   CG/LSCH   10 9 8 7 6 5 4 3 2 1

❖

First Edition

For my mom

CHAPTER 1

AT 7:54 IN THE MORNING, on a Friday, Mateo Flores punched Todd Morgan in the ear.

This was strange for three reasons:

1. Todd and Mateo were friends.
2. Mateo wasn't a violent person (off the middle school football field, at least).
3. Todd had very small ears for a twelve-year-old, making them unusually hard to hit.

Todd fell back into his bus seat, which he was sharing with Mateo. He cupped his tiny ear with his hand, moaning in pain.

"Why did you do that?" Todd asked, his ear ringing.

Mateo stared at his friend, looking confused. A

second later, a slow grin spread across his face. Slipping on his sunglasses, he stood up and jogged down the bus steps without a backward glance.

It was 7:56 in the morning.

The end of the world had already begun.

"That was weird."

In the seat across the aisle, Margot Blumenthal was watching Todd.

Margot was new to West Cove Middle School. She had blue-streaked hair, a perfect attendance record, and was considered a lock for the United States national freestyle wrestling team (as soon as she turned thirteen).

Even her teachers found her a little intimidating.

"Yeah," Todd agreed. "Weird. And, you know . . . painful."

Margot slid across the aisle and into Todd's seat, peering at his ear. "What happened?" she asked. "Did you guys get into a fight or something?"

"Uh, hello?" Todd leaned back, looking right at Margot. "Did I, like, invite you to sit with me?" Turning toward the window, he mumbled, "Weirdo" under his breath.

Margot stood up, rolling her eyes.

The bus was nearly empty now, the final students making their way down the steps. Margot reached into her pocket and pulled out a neatly folded surgical mask. "You should see the nurse," she told Todd, snapping the mask in place over her nose and mouth. "You could have a perforated eardrum."

As Todd pressed his hand to his ear in alarm, Margot hurried down the bus stairs and stepped onto the sidewalk. The scent of dead whale washed over her.

It was now 7:59 in the morning.

The end of the world was practically inevitable.

CHAPTER 2

THE DEAD WHALE, BY THE way, had nothing to do with the end of the world.

At least not yet.

The creature had been discovered several days ago by Mateo Flores's father, Rodrigo, during his evening jog on the beach. Rodrigo had called the local police, who, in turn, had contacted the National Oceanic and Atmospheric Administration.

The NOAA had sent several biologists to West Cove to gather samples from the whale and help plan its disposal. An adult male sperm whale, it measured close to fifty-eight feet long and was estimated to weigh forty-seven tons.

Obviously, it couldn't just be flushed down the toilet like a goldfish.

Instead, it would have to be lifted by crane from the ocean, and driven to a landfill on a semitrailer.

The crane, which was costing the town of West Cove a lot of money, was scheduled to arrive from Seattle later that night.

In the meantime, Margot hurried toward the middle school's entrance. The paper surgical mask she had slipped on in the bus filtered out the worst of the smell, but the heavy, oily stench still clung in the air, making her eyes water unpleasantly.

The girl in front of her, who Margot vaguely recognized from gym class, paused to hold the door open for her. "I think it's getting worse," she told Margot, her nose wrinkled in disgust.

"It's the methane," Margot explained through her mask. "The whale's decomposing, but its blubber and skin are trapping all the gaseous buildup."

Margot was the kind of girl who could use the word "gaseous" in conversation without blinking. She could also make an omelet in the traditional French style and recite the alphabet backward.

Yet more examples of her general impressiveness.

The girl let the door fall shut. "Whatever," she said, walking away from Margot as quickly as possible.

Margot pulled off her mask, briefly pausing to survey the main hallway. Her eyes landed on Mateo, who was standing on the opposite side of the hall, staring into his open locker.

Folding her mask in half, Margot watched him from a distance.

Despite what the earlier ear punch might imply, Mateo was actually a very likable person.

His friends liked him because he was fun, and easygoing, and usually had the newest Xbox games before anyone else.

His teachers liked him because he was polite, and hard-working, and almost always raised his hand in class (even when he didn't know the answer).

His coaches liked him because he left everything he had on the field during practice, and also regularly washed his workout clothes.

His dentist liked him because he flossed twice daily and never skipped a teeth cleaning.

Being liked was very important to Mateo.

It was so important to him, in fact, that in the six weeks she had spent rehearsing with him for the school play, Margot had never once seen him not smiling.

Which is why she kept watching as, halfway down the hallway, Mateo's mouth twisted into a frown. He slapped angrily at his back, just above his shoulder blades. A second later, he threw back his head and let out a frustrated scream.

A hundred conversations stopped. The corridor grew silent.

A long moment passed.

Mateo shook his head, clearing it. He looked around, seeming to realize for the first time where he was. His classmates stared curiously at him, waiting to see what he would do next.

Someone coughed.

Mateo forced himself to relax his shoulders, adopting his normal slouch. He pushed his sunglasses up on his head and gave a casual shrug. "Forgot my pencil," he said.

There was a beat, and then the laughter started.

Mateo grinned, shoving a passing friend good-naturedly. The hallway returned to normal, Mateo's joke soon forgotten in the rush of lost gym shoes and slamming lockers and last-minute copying of math homework.

Mateo pretended to look for something in his backpack, waiting until he was sure his classmates were no longer paying attention to him. Then, his grin fading, he closed his locker and slipped quietly down the hall.

Margot followed him.

CHAPTER 3

MATEO VEERED LEFT, INTO THE auditorium.

At first, Margot briefly wondered if she had blanked on a last-minute play rehearsal. But instead of heading for the stage, Mateo had ducked into one of the back-stage bathrooms.

That had been nearly five minutes ago.

"Mateo?" Margot knocked lightly on the door. "Are you in there? It's me, Margot."

There was silence from the other side of the door.

"Are you okay?" Margot called. "Because the final bell just rang."

"I'm fine," Mateo called back. "Thanks. All good!"

A thud echoed through the door.

8

"Mateo?"

"Nothing to worry about!" he yelled. "It's cool!"

Another thud echoed through the door, louder this time.

"Are you sure?" *Another* thud, this time followed by a series of grunts. "Mateo?" Margot knocked impatiently on the door. "Do you need me to get the nurse?"

"No! It's *fine!*" Mateo shouted. "I *mean* it!"

The next thud was so loud it shook the door frame. Margot narrowed her eyes. "Mateo?" She pulled on the handle, surprised to find that it opened. "Hang on!" she yelled. "I'm coming in!"

"No!" Mateo called, his voice panicked. "Don't!"

Margot pushed the door open and marched into the bathroom.

Mateo stood in front of the sink, gripping the edge of the counter with both hands. His sunglasses sat crooked on top of his head, as if they'd been accidentally knocked to the side. He was breathing heavily, and the back collar of his shirt was ripped. It looked like he'd been clawing at it.

Mateo was a fan of vintage polo shirts, particularly the pastel ones from the eighties with the little alligators on them. He usually took excellent care of them.

Mateo met Margot's gaze in the mirror, his eyes wide with panic. He took a shaky breath. "I think there might be something wrong with me."

Mateo was right; there *was* something wrong with him. Something very wrong indeed.

As Margot watched, something rippled beneath the collar of Mateo's shirt.

She tilted her head curiously to the side.

The "something" beneath Mateo's collar rippled again.

Margot tilted her head to the other side.

A goo-coated appendage pushed its way out of Mateo's collar, snaking slowly up his neck.

Margot's head snapped straight up.

"Is that a *tentacle*?" she asked.

"I don't know. It feels weird," Mateo told her, twitching slightly. "And my brain is, like, all foggy or something. Like I can't even rememb—" He stopped suddenly, his back stiffening.

A vacant grin spread across his face.

Margot took a step back. She was beginning to suspect she was in over her head. "Why don't I go get someone?" she asked. "They can . . . help."

Mateo's grin widened.

"Just wait here," Margot said, reaching for the door handle. "Don't move, okay? I'll—"

Mateo let out a snarl. Lowering his shoulders, he rushed her.

Years of training took over. Shifting automatically into a neutral wrestling pose, Margot positioned her head, arms, and hips into three separate lines of defense.

The entire incident was over in less than a minute.

Stepping forward to meet Mateo, Margot rotated her body inward. Pulling his arm across her waist, she turned, using her handhold to catch his head in her armpit. She fell backward, locking her grip around his head and arm.

It was a near perfect headlock.

"What is *wrong* with you?" Margot demanded, tightening her hold around Mateo's neck.

"I'm sorry," he wheezed, blinking apologetically up at her. "It wasn't *me*, okay?" With his free hand, Mateo tugged the back of his pink-and-green striped shirt down as far as he could. "Look," he begged Margot. "Just look!"

Margot looked.

To her credit, she didn't even scream.

CHAPTER 4

"WHAT DO YOU THINK IT is?" Mateo twisted his neck uselessly back and forth, trying to look between his shoulder blades.

Margot stared down at the creature, thoughtfully narrowing her eyes.

"A leech?" she asked. "I did a report on the Amazon leech once. It can grow to be up to eighteen inches long." She paused for a second. "You haven't been to the Amazon lately, have you?"

"Um, no?"

She shook her head. "Probably not an Amazon leech then. Besides, leeches don't have tentacles."

Margot leaned forward, examining the squirming

creature attached to the skin at the top of Mateo's back more closely. There didn't seem to be a head, which was strange and a little alarming. Equally alarming were the four wriggling tentacles and the fact that, beneath its coating of yellow goo, the creature's skin was bright blue.

It was also glowing.

"We should get an adult," Margot said.

"Yeah." Mateo took a deep breath. "Probably."

"Okay. So . . . I'm going to let go of you now, I guess?" Margot asked.

With her arms wrapped around him, she couldn't help noticing how nice Mateo smelled. Like . . . lemon-scented floor polish.

Actually, Margot realized, it probably *was* lemon-scented floor polish. They were, after all, lying on the bathroom floor.

She cleared her throat, suddenly insecure about how close they were to each other. Was her deodorant still working? Could Mateo tell how fast her heart was beating? What if he could see up her *nose*?

"You're going to be calm, right?" she asked.

"Uh-huh," Mateo said, attempting to nod. "I mean, I'll try."

"Don't try," Margot said firmly, quoting her dad. "*Do.*"

Mateo blinked. "Right. I'll be calm."

Cautiously releasing her grip, Margot scooted away from him. Mateo sat up straight, rolling his neck around a couple of times to loosen his muscles.

"You're pretty good at that," he told Margot. "Wrestling."

Margot, in fact, was not "pretty good" at wrestling.

She was exceptional at it.

Her father, Leo Blumenthal, was a well-known professional wrestling coach and owner of the illustrious Blumenthal Wrestling Academy. Over the years, his academy had produced countless state champions, six world champions, and not one, but two Olympic bronze medalists.

Margot was his most promising student in years.

She shrugged. "Yeah, I guess." Margot didn't like to talk about wrestling.

"Sorry about the whole . . . attacking you . . . thing," Mateo said. "That was weird, right?" He gave a strange, high-pitched laugh, the sound echoing loudly in the small room. His eyes seemed brighter than usual, Margot noticed. Almost *too* bright.

She wondered if Mateo was in shock.

She wondered if *she* was in shock.

Margot didn't *feel* like she was in shock. But then again, it was hard to tell with all the adrenaline pumping through her body.

Had her mouth *always* tasted like metal?

"How do you feel?" she asked Mateo, sitting back on her heels. "Do you think you can make it to the nurse's office? Is that a bad idea? Should I lock you in here instead?"

"No! Don't leave me alone!" Mateo swallowed. "I mean, um, I can go with you. I'll be fine, I swear." The edge of fear in his voice made him sound younger than usual. "What do you think it *is*?" he asked again.

"It *could* be a leech," Margot offered dubiously. "A mutation, maybe? Have you been near any lakes lately? Or a tide pool?"

Mateo thought for a second. "I don't think so?"

Margot pursed her lips, thinking. "I wonder how long it's been on you."

"I don't know," Mateo said. "I don't think it was there yesterday, though. I mean, I didn't feel weird or anything."

Margot stood up. "I guess it doesn't matter right now. We should go see the nurse." She took a hair tie from her pocket and pulled her loose hair into a ponytail. Her blue streaks were especially noticeable in the fluorescent lights.

Her eyes fell on the mop leaning against the wall in the corner. Striding forward, she picked it up and

15

twisted the base free. Hefting the handle in front of her, she motioned toward the door. "You first."

Mateo stared at her. "Um . . . do I want to know what that's for?"

"For hitting you with," Margot told him. She swung the mop handle through the air, pretending to crash it down on his back. "Just in case," she added to reassure him.

Mateo stared at her. "Oh. Solid plan."

If Margot had been someone who blushed easily, she would have blushed.

Mateo took a shaky breath then pushed himself to his feet. He glanced automatically in the mirror, checking to make sure his sunglasses weren't broken, then straightened them on top of his head. "Okay," he said, staring queasily at his reflection. "I'm ready."

Slinging the mop handle over her shoulder, Margot lifted her chin. "Let's go."

CHAPTER 5

EARLIER THAT MORNING, ACROSS TOWN, Dr. Smalls was not having a good day.

A lumpy mattress had kept him up most of the night. He had spilled orange juice on his tie. And he was still four hundred and eighty-seven days away from retirement.

"Good morning!" Calvin Biggs, Dr. Smalls's research assistant, strode cheerfully into the conference room. He set a steaming takeout cup of coffee down on the table in front of his boss. "Half-caf, soy milk, no-whip cappuccino," he said. "With a sprinkle of cinnamon on top." He placed a paper bag next to the coffee. "They were out of croissants, so I picked you up a muffin instead."

"What kind?" Dr. Smalls asked, his eyes narrowing.

"Er, I don't know," Calvin admitted. "It was the last one they had."

Dr. Smalls grunted. He pulled the muffin out of the bag, examining it suspiciously.

Was it banana nut? Was it pumpkin? Was it *bran*?

Pushing the muffin aside, he reached for his cappuccino.

Calvin waited until his boss had taken his first sip then gave him an encouraging smile. "Sleep any better last night?" Calvin asked hopefully.

Dr. Smalls gave another grunt in reply. "Just got off the phone with Seattle," he said. "They want us to wrap things up by tomorrow. Not soon enough in my opinion."

He glared around the Cozy Inn's multipurpose lounge as though the upholstered armchairs and polished tables had somehow offended him.

Calvin subtly checked his watch.

"Do you want a ride to the school?" he asked.

Dr. Smalls peered up at him with a vacant expression. "The school?"

"You agreed to give a talk at the local middle school?" Calvin reminded his boss. "About the importance of ocean conservation?"

Dr. Smalls eyed the muffin again. Could it be oatmeal raisin?

"I'm afraid you'll have to do it, Biggs," he said firmly, not meeting his assistant's gaze. "I'm absolutely swamped with these data charts. Couldn't possibly slip away."

Calvin's eyes flicked briefly toward the doctor's open laptop. A half-played game of solitaire was clearly visible on the screen.

Dr. Smalls snapped his computer shut.

Calvin tugged uneasily at his hair. He was good at many things, including but not limited to: jigsaw puzzles, urban gardening, competitive chili cook-offs, and remembering people's phone numbers.

He was *not* good at public speaking.

"Okay. Sure," he said. "I guess if things don't go well I can always show that video of the six-hundred-pound octopus squeezing through the tube, right? Kids like that."

Dr. Smalls gave a dismissive wave. "Sure, sure, whatever. Just bring back lunch, will you?" Visions of octopus floated through his head. "Sushi, if you can find it."

Four hundred and eighty-seven days, Calvin reminded himself. *Only four hundred and eighty-seven days until Dr. Smalls's retirement.*

"I'm not sure if West Cove has a sushi restaurant," he said aloud. "But I'll check."

Dr. Smalls, who had already lost interest in the conversation, gave another grunt in reply. He waited impatiently for Calvin to leave before flipping open his computer. Squinting down at the screen, he sucked thoughtfully at his teeth. Where was that king of clubs hiding, anyway?

He absently took a bite of muffin, sputtering a little as a dry piece hit his tongue.

It was bran.

CHAPTER 6

"DO YOU REALLY NEED TO keep pointing that thing at me?" Mateo asked, glancing nervously at Margot.

Their footsteps fell softly on the carpet of the empty hallway. The rest of school had been in class for almost twenty minutes.

Margot lowered the mop handle. A little. "Sorry," she told Mateo. "Just a precaution."

Mateo tugged uneasily at the collar of his polo shirt, shuddering. "I guess it's not like I blame you." He started to turn his neck, trying once again to look between his shoulder blades, then thought better of it. "Hey, do you think this . . . thing . . . means I'll be able to leave school early?" he asked, making a feeble attempt at a joke.

"We have that quiz in geometry today."

"Probably," Margot said. "I suppose we'll have to cancel the play tonight, too. Unless Mrs. Fournier wants to add a scene where Juliet puts Romeo in a half nelson." She gave a small, disappointed sigh.

Romeo and Juliet was, perhaps, an odd choice for a middle school play, but the director had been unable to resist after finding the sets and costumes online for cheap.

Mrs. Fournier was both thrifty *and* a romantic at heart.

She was also extremely practical, which is why she had heavily edited the script for both length and content.

Margot straightened her shoulders. "Anyway, let's get you to the nurse," she said.

"Sorry. Yeah," Mateo said, wiping his sweaty palms on his jeans. "Okay."

They lapsed into silence, their pace quickening as they neared the nurse's office. When they rounded the corner, they narrowly avoided running into Luke Besserman, who was just pushing his wheelchair out of the bathroom.

"What's up, man?" Luke asked Mateo. He flicked his gaze curiously at Margot, who attempted to casually rest the mop handle on her shoulder. "What are you guys doing?"

"Nothing," Mateo said. "Just . . . play stuff."

"*Romeo and Juliet*," Margot added. "By William Shakespeare."

"Yeah, I know who it's by," Luke said, giving her a strange look. "Everyone does." His eyes moved to Mateo's torn collar. "You okay, dude?"

"Yeah," Mateo said quickly. "Totally."

"Are you sure?" Luke asked. He leaned forward a little, peering up at Mateo more closely. "Because you've got, like, some scratches or something on your neck."

Beneath Mateo's shirt, the goo-coated creature rippled slightly.

Mateo's head jerked in response.

Margot stiffened, tightening her grip on the mop handle.

Mateo balled his hands into fists and shoved them into his pockets. "Anyway," he said tightly. "We should get going. We've got a lot of . . ."

"Play stuff," Margot reminded him. "We've got a lot of play stuff to do. For the play."

"Right," Mateo said, his voice strained. His head gave another jerk, and he took a step in Luke's direction. "Play stuff."

23

Margot grabbed him by the wrist before he could get closer to Luke. "See you later, Luke," she said, yanking Mateo into the nearest doorway.

Luke stared after them. "You know that's a bathroom, right?"

"Play stuff!" Margot called back, swinging the door shut behind them.

Luke leaned back in his wheelchair for a moment, drumming his fingers against the wooden hall pass in his lap.

"Weirdo," he muttered, then shrugged and headed toward class.

CHAPTER 7

"MATEO?" MARGOT ASKED INSIDE THE bathroom. She pointed her mop handle in his direction. "Are you okay?"

Mateo grinned in response.

It wasn't a friendly grin.

"I'm warning you," Margot said. She nodded toward the mop handle. "I'm not afraid to use this thing."

Mateo's unfriendly smile widened.

As he charged toward her, Margot swung the mop handle through the air. Unexpectedly, she went low, sweeping Mateo's feet from beneath him.

Mateo's momentum carried him forward as he fell to the ground, arms flailing.

It is at this moment that most twelve-year-olds would have hesitated.

Margot, however, did not.

Grabbing a handful of paper towels from the nearest dispenser, she knelt next to Mateo, rolling him all the way over on his stomach. He groaned in protest.

Margot ignored him.

With her left hand, she lowered the torn collar of Mateo's polo shirt, exposing the glowing, leechlike creature attached to his back.

Margot flinched.

Then, steeling herself, she drew a deep breath. Using the paper towels as a kind of protective barrier, she clamped her hand over the creature.

It was unpleasantly squishy. Not to mention oddly cold to the touch, even through the paper towels.

"Ready?" Margot asked Mateo.

He turned his head, gazing blearily up at her. "What? No!"

"One," Margot counted.

"Wait," Mateo said, beginning to panic. "Just wait for a second!"

"Two."

Margot's fingers tightened around the creature. She yanked with all her strength. Its body stretched like a piece of Silly Putty.

Mateo cried out in alarm. Squeezing his eyes shut, he pressed his forehead against the bathroom floor.

Margot narrowed her gaze.

Still clutching the creature, she stood up. Bracing one foot against the small of Mateo's back, she jerked her arm backward, wrenching it over her shoulder.

The creature finally broke free with a sucking noise.

Startled, Margot let go. It flew through the air and over her head, smacking with a wet sound against the bathroom wall.

The creature lurched toward the floor drain beneath the sink, its body squelching softly against the tile.

"We should try to—"

"Just let it go," Mateo said firmly. He eased into a sitting position, his eyes wary.

The pulsating, electric-blue creature flattened itself over the drain. As Margot and Mateo watched, unmoving, it slowly squeezed its entire body through one of the grate's tiny holes, disappearing into the drain itself.

Margot and Mateo stared at the drain in disbelief.

"Well," Margot said. "That was . . . interesting."

Another wave of adrenaline flooded through her veins, making everything seem louder and brighter and more intense. It was the same way she'd felt right after she'd pinned Derek Adams in the state finals, back in Iowa.

Well, almost the same way.

Margot dropped the now slimy paper towels into the trash can. Stepping up to the sink, she began to wash her hands.

Mateo stared at her.

"Interesting?"

Margot concentrated on her hands, making sure to soap in between her fingers. "*Very* interesting?" she asked.

Mateo climbed slowly to his feet. "You could have warned me," he said accusingly.

Margot scrubbed beneath her fingernails so hard that it made her wince. "I counted to three," she pointed out.

"*Two*," Mateo said. "You counted to *two*." He turned away from the mirror, trying to catch a glimpse of his back. "Is it all gone? There aren't any, like, pieces left or anything, are there?"

Margot took a slow breath, calming her nerves. She pulled a paper towel free from the dispenser then turned to examine Mateo's back. The only remaining sign of the creature were two small reddened patches of skin and a smear of quickly drying yellow goo.

She leaned closer. The floor polish smell was gone, replaced by something fruitier.

"Do you use mango shampoo?" she asked.

"What?" Mateo looked up in confusion.

"Never mind," Margot said quickly. "Here, wait a second." Wetting the paper towel, she added soap then handed it to Mateo.

Shuddering, he cleaned the goo from his upper back. "Did I get it all?"

Margot checked. "Yeah, I think so."

With hands that shook just slightly, she reached up to tighten her ponytail. "Come on," she said. "We should still go to the nurse's office."

"The nurse?" Mateo shook his head. "Uh-uh. I'm not going to the nurse."

"But . . . you have to. We don't even know what that thing was. What if it's poisonous? Or worse?"

Mateo raised his eyebrows. "Worse than poisonous?"

"You know what I mean," Margot said.

Mateo dropped his gaze, plucking at the torn collar of his polo shirt in annoyance. "Bogus," he muttered. "I really liked this one."

"Mateo," Margot said.

He purposefully didn't look at her. "It was forty bucks on eBay," he said. "You see how the alligator is blue? Do you know how rare that is?"

"Forget your shirt," Margot ordered him. "You need to be checked out by a medical professional!"

Mateo kept staring at the collar of his shirt, hesitating.

29

Margot could tell that he was wavering. But before she could fully convince him, the bell rang.

Mateo glanced around the bathroom as if he'd just realized where he was. He shook his head, clearing it. "Honestly, I'm fine. And I mean, the thing's gone, anyway, right? So let's just . . . forget about it. Okay?" A smile appeared out of nowhere, camouflaging any doubts he might have still had.

"But . . ." Margot said.

For once, she was at a loss for words.

Mateo opened the bathroom door and stepped outside. Margot followed him into the hallway, which was already flooding with noise as their classmates spilled out of their first-period classrooms.

"Hey, thanks, by the way," Mateo said, pausing in front of the door. "You were awesome. Really." Flashing her another smile, he slipped into the crowd.

Margot was still staring after him when the bathroom door swung open behind her, thudding against the heels of her sneakers.

"Ow!"

Catching her balance, Margot turned to see Calvin Biggs grimacing apologetically in the doorway.

"Er, sorry about that," he said. "I guess you probably thought the bathroom was empty, huh?"

CHAPTER 8

"ANYWAY, SORRY, SORRY, I DIDN'T mean to scare you," Calvin told Margot apologetically, glancing around the busy hallway. "I didn't think you'd be, you know, right outside the door."

Margot narrowed her gaze. Grabbing Calvin by the sleeve, she pulled him around the corner, away from the lockers. "You were in there the whole time?" she demanded. "What did you see? Wait, who even *are* you?"

Calvin scrubbed a freshly sanitized hand through his hair. "I'm Calvin. Calvin Biggs. From the National Oceanic A—"

"The National Oceanic and Atmospheric Administration," Margot finished for him. "You're supposed to be giving a talk today."

"Actually, it's my boss who's supposed to be giving the talk," Calvin said. "He sent me because he was . . ." Calvin momentarily paused, trying to think of the most tactful way to put it. "Busy. Anyway, I'm not, uh, I'm not real big on public speaking, so I went to the bathroom to . . ."

Margot raised her eyebrows.

"*Prepare*," Calvin said. "Mentally prepare. Only then you guys came in and . . . well." A fascinated look spread across his face. "I've never seen anything like that before. It's still there, in the drain, you know. I could see a sort of . . . glow." He shook his head, thinking aloud. "It must be an invertebrate, to have been able to fit through the grate. You didn't feel any bones, did you? When you handled it?"

"No." An involuntary shudder ran through Margot as she remembered the feeling of icy wetness seeping through the paper towels. "No bones. It just sort of . . . oozed . . . through the grate."

Calvin nodded. "I'm guessing it might be an undiscovered species of cephalopod. Without a shell or vertebrae to limit them, they can squeeze through some pretty tight spots."

It was Margot's turn to nod. "Like octopuses," she said.

"Exactly!" Calvin looked at her in appreciation. "You know, I could show you a video of a six-hundred-pound one squeezing through a tube that you wouldn't even believe."

"Maybe later," Margot said.

"Right. Sorry." A couple of students turned the corner, heading for the art room. Calvin waited until they passed, then lowered his voice. "Anyway, I unscrewed the grate, but it's pretty small. My hands were too big to reach, so I was just heading out to the van to try to find something to pry it out with. Although . . ."

He tilted his head to the side, looking speculatively at Margot's hands.

"Seriously?" Margot asked.

"You're right," Calvin said, shaking his head. "Sorry, no, of course not. I don't know what I was thinking." He ran his fingers through his hair again, tugging thoughtfully at a tuft just above his ear. "I can probably jerry-rig one of the suction samplers off a submersible to fit inside the drain," he said, thinking aloud. "Or I might have a pair of stray aquarium tongs somewhere. Although who knows how long we have? It was still in the trap when I left, but if it heads down the drain line . . . well . . ." He shot another furtive look at Margot's hands.

She closed her eyes for a moment, letting out a heavy sigh. "Fine."

Calvin's head popped up. "Yeah?" he asked in excitement. "Really? That's awesome. You're not going to regret this, I swear." He took an eager step in the direction of the bathroom.

"Uh, where do you think you're going?" Margot asked.

Calvin paused, his forehead wrinkling in confusion as he turned back to look at Margot. "To the bathroom," he said. "I'm going to help."

Margot pushed up the sleeves of her hoodie. "Yeah," she said. "No offense, but I work better alone. If you want to help, watch the door."

"But . . . are you sure?" Calvin asked.

Margot shrugged. "Usually."

Slipping around the corner, she ducked back into the bathroom. A quick glance beneath the stall doors assured her that the bathroom was empty. For real, this time.

She crossed to the floor drain, underneath the sink, peering down at the open grate. Calvin was right; there was a faint, bluish glow coming from the drain.

The creature was definitely still in there.

Outside, the bell rang, signaling the start to second period.

Margot closed her eyes, breathing slowly in through her nose.

It was a technique her father had taught her to use before wrestling matches.

She would picture herself pinning her opponent to the mat with quick, sure movements. No wasted energy. No mistakes. Just a clean, controlled victory.

It was a less effective technique when it came to pulling a mysterious, slimy creature from a public restroom floor drain, she discovered.

Margot opened her eyes.

"One," she counted aloud to herself, stepping forward. "Two."

And, before she could get to three, she dropped to her knees, thrusting her arm into the hole.

Margot cringed as her fingertips brushed against the cold, slimy surface of the creature.

Straining forward, she managed to close her fingers around the slippery mass. She pulled her arm back, tugging until the creature broke free of the drain with a loud *squelch*.

Wrinkling her nose in disgust, she held it out at arm's length.

Striding quickly across the bathroom, she shouldered open the door and checked to make sure the hallway was empty.

Calvin gave her an expectant look. "Well?" he asked.

Margot stepped through the door, holding the creature aloft in response.

"Awesome," Calvin breathed, staring at the pulsating, goo-coated . . . thing . . . wriggling in Margot's grasp. "Way to go, er . . ." He broke his gaze away from the creature to look up at her. "I just realized I don't know your name," he said.

A drop of yellow goo splattered the tip of Margot's shoe.

She narrowed her eyes, looking disapprovingly at the squirming creature in her hand.

"It's Margot," she told Calvin, lifting her chin. "Margot Blumenthal."

CHAPTER 9

A FEW MINUTES LATER, MARGOT paced nervously in front of her science classroom's door, while Calvin bent low over a microscope. "Aren't you supposed to be in class right now?" Calvin asked. "You're not going to get in trouble, are you?"

Margot shook her head. "We're supposed to be having an assembly," she pointed out. "Everyone's in the auditorium, waiting for your speech."

"Oh." Calvin examined the sample of yellow goo he had placed on the slide. "Right," he said distractedly. "There isn't by chance a scanning electron microscope tucked away in one of these cupboards, is there?"

Margot looked around at the sixth-grade science classroom.

"I think Mrs. Rothmann might have Twizzlers hidden in her desk," she offered.

"Never mind." Calvin leaned forward, pressing his forehead against the scope. "This is unbelievable," he breathed. "I've never seen anything like this before in my life."

"So it *is* a new species?" Margot asked.

She glanced at the creature she had pulled from the drain, which was now safely secured inside the glass aquarium the class had used to grow tadpoles in earlier that year.

Margot had piled a stack of textbooks on top of the aquarium's lid, just to be on the safe side.

Calvin didn't seem to hear the question. "The mucus that coats most cephalopods is made of a mix of water and long strands of protein," he said. "What I'm seeing here isn't protein." He looked up from the microscope lens, shaking his head slowly back and forth. "I'm not sure *what* it is."

"Can I see?" Margot asked. Calvin stepped to the side, and Margot took his place at the microscope, her ponytail falling against her cheek as she bent low.

A swarm of bright yellow, disk-shaped cells swam in front of her eyes, each one of them covered in what looked like hundreds of pyramid-like points.

Margot lifted her eyes from the microscope, glancing over at the aquarium again. The glowing, blue-skinned creature pressed wetly against the side, smearing the glass with thick goo.

For some reason, she felt a nervous tug at her stomach.

"Maybe it's a new kind of mucus," she offered.

Calvin reached up, tugging thoughtfully at his hair again. "Maybe," he mused. "But I've never seen a cellular structure like this before. Anywhere. Ever. Does your friend know how he managed to get it attached to himself in the first place?"

"He's not my friend," Margot said promptly. "And no. He doesn't even know how long it was on him."

Calvin looked disgruntled. Nudging Margot out of the way, he took his place back at the microscope. Margot sat down at the nearest desk, glancing uneasily at the aquarium again. She pulled out her phone.

As Calvin muttered quietly to himself, Margot began to search.

The closest she could come to matching the creature they had pulled from Mateo's back was the ribbon eel, a species of moray eel that looked a little bit like a mythical Chinese dragon.

Margot paused.

She stared down at her phone for a long moment.

Then, feeling slightly ridiculous, she added the word "alien" to her search.

A link to the website conspiracyproject.com appeared. Margot tapped on it, her stomach tugging nervously again.

The website was run by a former lifeguard who claimed to have had an alien encounter a few years ago. The lifeguard, Rolly Valverde, described a blue, goo-covered creature that had attached itself to his spine, causing him to act strangely until it was removed.

There were a handful of comments from people who claimed to have had similar experiences with an alien creature.

One woman had attacked her son's karate teacher for no reason. Another man had punched his best friend in the stomach. "CatLover88" had actually ended up in jail after assaulting half a dozen Pizza Ranch employees with a pair of salad tongs.

Any other day, Margot would have dismissed the website as ridiculous.

But today was not like other days.

Her limbs felt suddenly weightless, as though they might just float away.

"Um, Calvin?" she asked. "You might want to look at this."

"Hmm?" Calvin asked, distracted. "Look at what?"

"My phone," Margot told him. "There's something on my phone you need to see."

"In a sec," he said.

"Now," Margot said, her voice firm. "You need to look at this *now*."

Calvin pulled back from the microscope, blinking up at her in surprise. Wordlessly, Margot handed him her phone.

Calvin looked down at the screen.

His forehead wrinkling, he started to read.

When he looked up a moment later, his eyes were wide.

Margot stared at him.

He stared at Margot.

"Well . . ." Calvin said at last. "That's interesting."

CHAPTER 10

MARGOT PACED BACK AND FORTH in front of Mateo's locker, anxiously drumming her fingers against her crossed arms.

The hallways were noisier than usual, swarming with students who had just been released from the auditorium. Calvin, of course, had never shown up to give his speech; like Margot, he had been too busy discovering an alien species. Margot's eyes swept back and forth through the crowd, searching for Mateo. Acutely aware of the fact she had just missed her first two class periods, she also kept a wary eye out for teachers.

"Hey." A few lockers down from Mateo's, Chelsea Mandetti shut her door, giving Margot a curious look.

"What's up?" she asked, flipping her curly hair over her shoulder. "Are you waiting for Mateo or something?"

Forcing herself to stop pacing, Margot turned to look at Chelsea.

Although they'd been rehearsing together for over a month (Chelsea had been cast as the nurse in *Romeo and Juliet*), Margot didn't know her well.

To be fair, she didn't know *anyone* well.

Margot had never had much time for friends. Besides, they were a distraction.

Or at least that's what her father had always told her.

"Yeah," Margot said. "Kind of. We just have some . . . play stuff . . . to talk about."

Chelsea tilted her head to the side, looking curiously at her. "What kind of play stuff? Are you guys going to run lines or something? Because I'd be into that."

"No!" Margot practically shouted.

Chelsea drew back in alarm, her eyes widening.

"I mean, we're not running lines," Margot said, dropping her voice. "I just wanted to talk to him. About . . . stuff."

"Stuff," Chelsea repeated.

"Yep!" Margot said. "Stuff!" She gave a strained smile, her eyes darting over Chelsea's shoulders to look for Mateo.

"Are you okay?" Chelsea asked. "You look a little weird."

"I'm fine. Totally fine. Great, even," Margot said quickly. "I'm just . . . nervous," she improvised. "About tonight."

"Please," Chelsea said. "You've had everything memorized for, like, three weeks. You're going to be fine." She made a face. "If anyone chokes, it's going to be Mateo. Yesterday I saw him writing his lines down on his arm so he wouldn't forget them."

Margot caught a glimpse of Mateo as he turned the corner into the hallway. He was walking alongside Todd, the two of them joking around as though the ear punch earlier that morning had never even happened.

Boys were strange like that, Margot thought, forgetting all about Chelsea. Pushing herself up on her toes, she called out, "Mateo!" and waved her arms.

Mateo's pace slowed as he caught sight of Margot standing next to his locker. For a moment, it looked as though he was about to turn and run.

"Oh, hey, man, by the way, Brutus got ahold of that new *Halo* game you lent me," Todd said. He bared his teeth like a dog, shaking his head back and forth and growling. "It was vicious. Sorry, bro, but it's pretty much toast. I, like, owe you one, or whatever."

Thumping Mateo on the shoulder, Todd peeled

away, heading for his locker on the other side of the hallway. Mateo fixed his grin into place and forced himself forward.

"What's up?" he asked Margot as casually as he could. Giving a nod in Chelsea's direction, he stepped up to his locker and began twisting open his combination lock.

Margot stepped forward as well, lowering her voice. "We need to talk," she said. "About . . . *you know*," she added meaningfully.

Chelsea glanced curiously between Mateo and Margot.

Mateo spun his lock to number forty-six. "Can it wait?" he asked. "The bell's about to ring."

"It'll be fast," Margot lied. "I promise."

He twisted his lock in the other direction, coming to rest on number twenty-three.

"I just thought we were done," Mateo said. "You know, with talking about it?"

"*Mateo*," Margot said. "Just trust me, okay? You're going to want to know about this."

Mateo's locker clicked open as he turned to number seventy-two. He looked away from the lock, reluctantly meeting Margot's gaze.

Margot raised her eyebrows, staring back at him.

Chelsea blinked.

"Uh, is there, like, something going on here?" she asked. "Because you guys are acting totally weird."

Margot ignored her. Sliding her phone a little bit out of her pocket, she nodded down at it with a meaningful look.

Mateo narrowed his eyes. "Fine," he said tightly. "But you'd better be right about this."

Margot lifted her chin. "I always am," she said simply.

"Right about what?" Chelsea asked, turning her head back and forth to look between them. "What are you guys talking about?"

Mateo finally glanced in Chelsea's direction. "It's nothing," he told her, struggling to keep a smile on his face. "Just . . . play stuff. We'll see you later, okay?"

He elbowed his locker closed, turning to Margot. She gave a quick nod, plunging into the stream of middle schoolers filling the hallway. Mateo reluctantly followed.

Chelsea stared after them. "But I'm in the play, too," she called in confusion. "Guys? I'm in the play, too!"

Margot and Mateo turned the corner without looking back.

CHAPTER 11

"THREE THINGS," MATEO SAID, LOOKING around. "One, why are we in a supply closet? Two, why is that . . . *thing* . . . in here with us?" He shuddered, pointing toward the aquarium that Calvin and Margot had stolen from the science classroom. "And three, who is this guy, anyway?"

Calvin cleared his throat, giving Mateo a little wave. "Calvin Biggs," he said. "Research assistant at the NOAA."

"The National Oceanic and Atmospheric Administration," Margot added helpfully.

Mateo blinked at her. "Yeah. That means nothing to me."

"He's the one who was supposed to be giving the speech this morning," Margot said.

"Technically, it was supposed to be my *boss* giving the speech," Calvin said. "Not that it matters," he added hastily, catching sight of Margot's expression.

"Uh-huh. Still nothing," Mateo said, crossing his arms.

"Oh. Er, right," Calvin said. "I was in the restroom earlier. I saw, well . . . everything. Or at least *heard* everything," he amended. "It was a little difficult to actually see from inside the bathroom stall."

Mateo stared at him. "So you were hiding in a middle school bathroom, spying on us?" he asked.

"What? No!" Calvin looked horrified. "I would never . . . I was just using the restroom and you came in!"

"The point is, he saw us. He saw the thing that was attached to your neck," Margot broke in impatiently, pointing toward the creature. "After you left, I went back in and pulled it out of the drain. We took it to the science lab so Calvin could examine it."

"Yeah? So?" Mateo asked belligerently. "What does this have to do with me?"

"Here," Margot said, thrusting her phone at him. "Just read this, okay?"

Mateo reluctantly took the phone from her. Calvin sat down on an overturned mop bucket to wait while

Margot shifted impatiently from one foot to the other.

Mateo had changed out of his ripped polo shirt, she noticed. The West Cove "Fightin' Sandpipers" T-shirt he had on now was all creased, as if it had been sitting at the bottom of his gym bag for a while.

It was strange to see him in a T-shirt, she realized. Like seeing your postman out of uniform at the grocery store.

"Well?" Margot asked as he scrolled to the bottom of the page. "Did you read the comments section?"

"Salad tongs?" Mateo asked. "Seriously?"

"I thought that was strange as well," Calvin offered.

Margot took her phone back. "It's the same thing," she told Mateo. "You have to admit, it's the same thing."

"Fine." He shrugged. "So it happened to some other people. What does that matter? It just *proves* it's not a big deal."

"Aliens," Margot said loudly. "This lifeguard guy is talking about *aliens*."

Mateo flinched.

"It's true," Calvin said. "Or at least, I think it is. Cephalopod mucus is usually comprised of a mixture of water and protein strands. But the coating on this creature is something entirely different. Just to begin with, the cellular structure—"

Mateo cut him off. "I don't need to hear the details,

okay?" He glanced uneasily toward the tadpole aquarium, suppressing a wave of nausea as he remembered the cold, slimy feeling against his spine.

"This *is* a big deal, okay?" Margot asked. "We need to tell someone. We need to tell a *lot* of people. I've already filled out an email on the website's contact form, just in case there's anything more this lifeguard guy can tell us, but we need to be thinking bigger. The police. The FBI. The *president*. We're talking about an *alien*, Mateo. And *we* discovered it."

Calvin cleared his throat. "I mean, technically, I was the one who suggested that we pull it from the drain," he murmured. "Just to put all of the facts out there."

Margot shot him an impatient look.

Mateo pulled off his sunglasses, nervously snapping them open and closed. "So?"

"So?" Margot repeated, staring at him in disbelief. "Are you serious? That's all you have to say? *So?*"

"You're not the one who had that *thing* sucking on your neck," Mateo shot back. "It's bad news, okay? Why couldn't you have just left it alone?"

As if it could sense them talking about it, the creature rippled its body inside the tank, leaving another thick smear of goo against the glass.

Margot turned away.

"I don't think you understand how big this is," she

said to Mateo. "I mean, this could be the most important scientific discovery since . . ."

"Ever," Calvin finished for her. "Since ever."

"I. Don't. Care," Mateo said, over enunciating each word. "I'm telling you, messing with this thing is a mistake." He slid his sunglasses back onto his head. "You guys do what you want. Just leave me out of it, okay?"

Margot drew back, oddly stung by his words. "Fine," she said. "If that's what you want. I just thought you'd want to know. But it's not like we need you or anything."

"Good," Mateo said, reaching for the door handle. "Then I'm leaving." But before his hand could close over it, the door swung open on its own.

Coach Jenkins stood in the hallway, peering curiously into the supply closet.

"Just what the heck is going on in here?" he asked.

CHAPTER 12

COACH JENKINS WAS THE KIND of man who, most mornings, woke with the dawn, enjoyed a brisk, seven-mile jog, rain or shine, and finished up with a delicious kale and wheatgrass smoothie for breakfast.

This morning, however, was different from most.

Coach Jenkins was tired. Large, dark circles ringed his eyes, and his skin hung from his jawline. He was listless. And, for some reason, he was much thirstier than usual.

He let the bags of salt he was carrying fall to the floor with a loud thump, jabbing his finger in Margot and Mateo's direction. "You two. The bell rang five minutes ago. Why aren't you in class? And *you*," he added, rounding on Calvin. "I'm pretty sure you're the so-called scientist everyone's spent the past forty minutes looking for. What the heck are you doing farting around in here?"

Calvin shifted guiltily on his bucket.

"Get out here, all of you," Coach Jenkins said. *"Go."*

Mateo, Margot, and Calvin dutifully filed out of the supply closet.

Even in his currently weakened state, Coach Jenkins still demanded respect.

In the hallway, Margot was the first to speak. "Mr. Jenkins, I know this looks . . . strange . . . but Mateo and I . . ." She glanced quickly in Mateo's direction then lifted her chin. "I mean, *Calvin* and I found something," she said. "We think it might be an alien. I know how it sounds, but we have proof! Just look inside the closet."

Calvin cleared his throat. "It's true," he said. "I've never seen anything like it before."

Next to Margot, Mateo's eyes suddenly widened.

"An alien, huh? That's a new one, I'll admit," Coach Jenkins said.

Mateo watched in horror as the back of Coach Jenkins's T-shirt rippled slowly.

"Still," Coach Jenkins said. "Stranger things have been known to happen." He blinked a couple of times, momentarily losing his train of thought.

There were marks on the side of his neck, Margot suddenly realized. They looked like scratches.

They *could be* cat scratches, of course. Margot's cat, Stampy, scratched her all the time.

Stampy had aggression issues. He was also depressed.

But the marks on Coach Jenkins's neck didn't look like cat scratches. They looked as though he'd been clawing at his neck.

Mateo raised a shaky hand, pointing at the coach's back. "Alien," he mouthed. *"Alien."*

Calvin and Margot looked at each other.

Coach Jenkins shook his head, clearing it. "Do any of you have any salt on you?" he asked out of nowhere. "We're going to need a lot of salt."

Margot and Mateo looked at each other.

Coach Jenkins peered down at the large bags of rock salt sitting at his feet. "Yep," he repeated, staring off into space. "I reckon we'll need a *heck* of a lot of salt."

Mateo and Calvin looked at each other.

"Salt," Coach Jenkins said. "Salt. Salt. Salt. You know, if you say it enough times, it kind of loses its meaning." He gave a philosophical shrug. "Oh, well."

Reaching down, he grabbed the handles of the rock salt bags. As he turned to leave, Margot and Calvin saw the telltale bump beneath his shirt.

"You kids get back to class," the coach said. "And you, Riggs, or whatever your name is, you might as well get up to the office and explain yourself. People have got better things to do than sitting around on their butts waiting for you, you know." He stared down at the bags of rock salt in his hands, looking momentarily startled to see them.

The alien creature beneath his shirt gave another wriggle.

Mateo took a half step back, bumping into the wall.

"Yes," Coach Jenkins said decisively. "Lots of things to do."

As the coach turned to leave, Margot elbowed Calvin in the side. "*Do* something," she mouthed to him.

Calvin held up his hands defensively. "Like what?" he mouthed back at her.

Margot elbowed him again, harder this time.

Calvin scowled at her, stepping forward.

"Er, Coach?" he asked. "I think you might . . . There might be . . . It's possible that you have a . . . On your back . . ." The scientist's words died in his mouth as Coach Jenkins turned slowly to face him, his expression dark.

"What did you say, son?" he asked in a dangerously quiet voice.

Calvin swallowed. "Er . . . I was just saying, there's a

small chance you may have . . . you know . . . an alien on your back."

Coach Jenkins's head twitched suddenly to the side. A second later, an unpleasant smile stretched across his face.

Dropping the bags of salt to the floor, he punched Calvin squarely in the face.

Calvin's eyes rolled back in his head. He fell to the ground, unmoving.

Coach Jenkins gave a satisfied nod. Picking up his salt, he strode purposefully down the hallway.

Margot was pretty sure she could hear him whistling.

CHAPTER 13

"I'M SORRY," MATEO SAID, POINTING down at Calvin's motion-less body. "Did Coach Jenkins just punch this guy's lights out?"

Margot knelt, checking Calvin's pulse. Still pulsing. "Yep."

"Okay, cool," Mateo said. "I thought I might be hal-lucinating."

"Nope," Margot said.

"Am I hallucinating about the part where Coach had an alien attached to him?" Mateo asked hopefully.

"Afraid not," Margot said.

"Right. Okay," Mateo said. "So aliens are real. Aliens are real and they're, like, invading us, or whatever.

Cool. That's cool. Cool, cool, cool, cool, cool."

"Are you okay?" Margot asked, sitting back on her heels and looking up at him in concern. "Try breathing through your nose." She demonstrated, inhaling deeply and blowing the breath out her mouth.

Mateo bent forward, clapping his hands on his knees. "I'll be fine," he said, staring at the floor. "I just need a second."

"Help now, panic later," Margot ordered. "Here, grab a leg."

Reaching down for one of Calvin's ankles, she began tugging him backward into the supply closet. His socks, she noted, were printed with tiny slices of flying pizza.

Mateo gingerly straightened up. Grasping Calvin's other ankle, he helped Margot pull the unconscious scientist into the tiny room.

Grunting with effort, Margot heaved Calvin into a sitting position, resting his head against the wall.

She tightened her ponytail, staring down at Calvin's limp body. A small stream of drool trickled down his chin.

"Okay," she said, thinking aloud. "Coach Jenkins is clearly . . . infected. Which means that *you* being infected *wasn't* an isolated incident. Which we already knew, because of that website."

"The lifeguard guy," Mateo said quickly. "Right.

Yeah. And the Pizza Ranch woman. Only Coach Jenkins didn't attack us right away," he pointed out. "And, you know, he didn't use salad tongs."

Margot began to pace back and forth in the closet, stepping over Calvin's feet. "You're right. He was fine when we were talking about aliens *in general*. It wasn't until Calvin mentioned the one on his back that he got . . . upset."

Mateo glanced down at Calvin's unmoving body. "That's one way of putting it," he said.

"Back in the bathroom," Margot said, continuing to pace as she thought aloud. "You didn't try to attack me until I mentioned seeing a tentacle. And in the hallway, you started growling at Luke when he noticed the scratches on your neck. What about earlier? On the bus?"

"The bus?" Mateo asked.

"When you punched Todd in the ear," Margot said impatiently. She lightly tapped her ear with her fist. "Remember?"

Mateo's forehead wrinkled. "I guess?" he asked. "It's all a little fuzzy. Or wait . . . the label! On my polo! Todd was grabbing for it. He kept saying it was a girl's shirt." He shook his head. "I like him, but that dude needs to work out his issues with the color pink."

"Focus," Margot ordered.

"Right," Mateo said. "Sorry. Hey, wait a sec," he said, realization dawning. "Are you saying that thing was, like, controlling me? Making me go all aggro every time it felt threatened or something?"

"Mind control." Margot quickened her pace. "It makes sense. Only, why? What are the aliens trying to *do*?"

Mateo bent his head over his knees again, trying not to hyperventilate.

"We still don't know how the two of you were infected to begin with," Margot said. "Mr. Jenkins is your football coach, right?" she prompted him. "Do you think that's when you got infected? During practice yesterday?"

"I didn't go to practice," Mateo reminded her. "We had play rehearsal, remember?"

"Right," Margot said. She bit her lip, trying to think. "Okay, so what did you do after rehearsal then?"

Mateo straightened. "I don't know. Nothing? Went home. Did homework. Messed around on the computer."

"Did you see anyone?" Margot prompted. "Or leave the house for any reason?"

"No. Dad brought takeout home after his meeting. We just ate it and went to bed."

Margot narrowed her eyes. "What meeting?"

"His conservation group. They used to never meet, but I guess Dad finding the whale got them all fired up again or something. This is, like, the third meeting in a row they've had."

"Who's in the group?" Margot demanded.

Mateo looked up at the ceiling, trying to remember. "Um, the mayor? She's his boss. And I think his squash partner, maybe? I don't really know."

Margot pulled her phone out of her pocket, and started typing quickly, searching for something.

"What are you doing?" Mateo asked.

Margot tapped on one of the results, turning the phone to face him. Mateo leaned forward, peering down at the screen.

It was a photo from that Tuesday's *West Cove Gazette*. Mateo's father, along with the rest of the West Cove Conservation Club, stood posed in front of the beached whale, attempting to smile through the smell.

"Local Environmentalists Give a Whale of an Effort," the headline read.

Margot pointed at the photo.

Standing directly next to Mateo's father, a baseball cap pulled low over his forehead, stood a burly man in a Windbreaker.

It was Coach Jenkins.

CHAPTER 14

MATEO'S EYES GREW WIDE.

"No. No, no, no, no, *no*." He pointed at the aquarium on the shelf, jabbing his finger insistently at the alien. "Are you telling me one of these suckers is attached to *my dad*?"

The question was still hanging in the air when the door to the supply closet swung open for the second time.

"Hey, I thought I heard you guys in here," Chelsea Mandetti said, resting her hip against the open door. "What are you . . ."

Her voice trailed slowly off as her gaze fell on the glass aquarium Mateo was still pointing at. The glowing, electric-blue alien thumped angrily against the side, smearing the glass with thick yellow goo.

Chelsea blinked.

She dropped her gaze to Calvin's slumped body, propped up against the wall.

She blinked again, harder this time.

"I thought you guys said you were doing play stuff."

Margot reached out, yanking Chelsea inside the closet and shutting the door firmly behind her. "Turn around," she demanded.

"What?" Chelsea said. "Why?"

Mateo lowered his hand, wiping his palms against his jeans. "Trust me," he told Chelsea. "It's for your own good."

"*What's* for my own good?" Chelsea asked. "What are you guys doing in here? Did you, like, *drug* that guy or something?" She pointed at Calvin.

Another trickle of saliva dripped from the scientist's chin.

"No!" Margot said.

"It was Coach Jenkins," Mateo offered. "He punched him in the face."

"Coach Jenkins?" Chelsea repeated. "Punched him . . ."

"In the face," Margot finished impatiently. "But that's the least of our problems right now." She crossed her arms against her chest. "Your back. Show it to us."

Chelsea glared at her. "Ugh, fine, if you're going to be all weird about it. Here," she said, whirling around to face the door. Chelsea gathered her thick, curly hair in both hands, lifting it above her neck. "There. Happy?"

Margot and Mateo leaned closer, examining the smooth slope of Chelsea's back beneath her T-shirt.

Margot nodded in satisfaction. "Yes."

Chelsea let her hair drop, spinning around to face them. "*Now* are you going to tell me what's going on?"

"Aliens are real," Margot said bluntly. "That thing in the aquarium is one of them."

Mateo shot her an annoyed look.

"What?" she asked. "That's what's going on."

Chelsea gave a nervous laugh, looking between Margot and Mateo. "No, but seriously. Tell me the truth, you guys."

Mateo sighed. "Margot's right," he said. "Aliens are real."

"This is one of them," Margot said, pointing at the aquarium. "We found it earlier, attached to Mateo's back. And this," she said, gesturing toward the slumped research assistant, "is Calvin Biggs. He's a scientist with the National Oceanic and Atmospheric Administration."

"One of the whale guys," Mateo added.

"Right," Margot said. "One of the whale guys. He's never seen anything like this thing before."

"So? That doesn't mean it's an alien," Chelsea pointed out. "I've never seen *lots* of things before."

"Fine," Mateo said. "Aliens *aren't* real. Happy?" He turned to Margot, his jaw tightening. "If you're right about my dad, we need to find him. Like, now." He reached nervously for his sunglasses then lowered his hand. "His office is at city hall. It's not far. We can walk."

Margot hesitated. "Okay. Yeah. Should we try to wake him up?" she asked dubiously, nodding toward Calvin. "He could have a concussion. Coach Jenkins hit him pretty hard."

"He's fine," Mateo said impatiently. "Football players get concussions all the time."

Margot wrinkled her nose. "Yeah, I'm pretty sure that's not a good thing." On the shelf next to Chelsea's shoulder, she spotted a box full of spare office supplies. "We can write him a note," she told Mateo, reaching for a pack of Post-its. "In case he wakes up before we get back."

"Fine," Mateo said. "Whatever. Let's just *go*."

Margot nodded. "One sec." She scribbled a couple of sentences down on the pad, then pulled the top sheet free and stuck it to Calvin's shirt. "Okay." Reaching up, she tightened her ponytail. "Ready."

"Um, you guys?" Chelsea asked. "This isn't funny anymore. We have *school*. You can't just . . . leave."

Mateo pulled open the door, stepping into the hallway. He waited impatiently for Margot, bouncing up and down on the soles of his sneakers.

"Wait!" Chelsea cried, hurrying out of the closet after them. "You're just going to leave the guy in there?" she asked. "With that . . . *thing*?"

Mateo swung the door shut with a loud click.

"We'll be back as soon as we can," Margot told Chelsea.

"What?!" Chelsea spluttered. "Come on, you're not seriously ditching, are you?"

"Sorry," Margot called unapologetically over her shoulder, jogging down the hallway after Mateo. "But the alien's contained. You'll be fine!"

"Aliens aren't real!" Chelsea cried in frustration.

Margot gave a final wave and turned the corner.

Chelsea was alone in the hallway.

CHAPTER 15

"I HOPE CALVIN'S OKAY," MARGOT said, hurrying to keep pace with Mateo. "What if he really *does* have a concussion?"

Mateo pushed his sunglasses up, not looking at her. "He'll be fine," he said shortly. "He's, like, a trained scientist, or whatever. Plus, we left him a note."

"I guess," Margot said dubiously, speeding up to catch Mateo.

The wind off the ocean was chilly, but the October sun was warm overhead as they hurried up the sharp inclines of West Cove's side streets. In the summer, West Cove was a bustling resort town; tourists poured in from all over the state to take pictures in front of the dramatic, rocky coastline and browse the overpriced gift stores.

The town's annual Sand Dollar Festival brought in over ten thousand people per year, and had even been featured on the Travel Channel before.

Margot, who had moved to West Cove at the beginning of August, liked the town much better in the fall. She liked the empty beaches and the smell of salt in the air and how loudly the waves crashed against the shoreline. She liked how everything felt so different from Iowa, the last place she'd lived. She even liked the taste of the vinegar potato chips sold in all the grocery stores.

In Iowa, she almost never ate potato chips.

It was fine, though.

Victory required sacrifice, as her dad liked to say.

She hurried up again, tightening her mask around her face. Even with everything else that was happening, the stench of dead whale could not be ignored.

"Do you think anyone's noticed we're gone yet?" she asked, changing the subject.

Sneaking out of school had been surprisingly easy; they had simply slipped out of the open back door.

Although Margot and Mateo weren't aware of the fact, it was Coach Jenkins who had accidentally left the door propped open when he had left with his bags of salt.

He had also left the light on in his office.

Mateo shrugged. "I don't know. Maybe?"

Margot thought wistfully of her previously perfect attendance record. But, she told herself sternly, an alien invasion was more important.

"So your dad's a city planner?" she asked, changing the subject yet again.

"Yeah." Mateo started walking even faster. Margot was practically running to keep up with him.

"What about your mom?" Margot panted as they passed one of West Cove's many ice-cream shops. It was empty, its windows shuttered for the season. "Do you think she could be infected, too?"

"Probably not," Mateo said. "Seeing as how she's dead and everything."

Margot stumbled on a smooth patch of sidewalk.

"It was a long time ago," Mateo said, not looking at her. "When I was little. It's fine."

It wasn't fine.

Losing a parent is never fine.

Still, Margot nodded. She didn't know what else to do.

"What about your parents?" Mateo asked. "Are you worried about them?"

Margot shook her head. "My mom left for Olympia this morning. This work thing. She's not getting back until tonight. And my dad is . . . he's still in Iowa. For now," she added quickly. "He's coming out as soon as he can."

"He's your wrestling coach, too, right? Your dad?"

Margot looked up in surprise. "How did you know that?"

He shrugged. "I don't know. I saw this thing online about you after you moved here. You're kind of a big deal."

"Oh," Margot said. "Yeah. I guess."

"So are you going to, like, join the wrestling team here? Or is your dad just going to coach you?"

"I don't know." Margot glanced over at him. "I have a spot on Team USA when I turn thirteen next month. If I want it."

"Whoa," Mateo said. "Like, traveling to international competitions, and everything? That's awesome."

A sudden sick feeling pushed its way into Margot's stomach.

"Yeah," she said. "I guess. I don't know. I mean, it's what I've been working for my entire life."

The sick feeling crept its way up toward her throat.

Margot pointed toward the large, beige building on

the corner across the street. The sign out front read "West Cove City Hall."

"Is that it?" she asked, pushing her nausea away.

Mateo looked up, sucking in his breath. "Yeah," he said shortly. "It is. Here we go."

CHAPTER 16

MATEO HELD THE DOOR OPEN for Margot, bouncing nervously up and down on the soles of his feet again.

"Okay," he said, pushing his sunglasses onto his head. "This is going to be okay, right? I mean, he's probably not even infected."

Margot nodded reassuringly. She was almost 100 percent sure that Mateo's father was infected.

"It'll be fine," she said, pulling off her mask. "Even if he is, we can just, you know . . ." She mimed a quick yanking motion, clicking her tongue for effect.

Mateo looked a little queasy as he turned and led the way toward his father's office.

The interior of city hall was expensive-looking, with

light gray walls and polished wood floors. Realistic-looking plastic plants were dotted throughout the hallway, and the air smelled faintly of berry-scented air freshener. Muzak played softly in the background.

It was, on most days, probably a pleasant place to work.

Mateo's father's office was halfway down the hallway, on the left. A small plaque on the door read "Rodrigo Flores: City Planner."

Mateo paused outside the door, gathering his courage.

Margot, who wasn't sure what they were about to find behind the door, shifted into a defensive stance, squaring her back and bending her knees.

Mateo gave her a look.

"Sorry," Margot said. "Habit."

She straightened up. Slightly.

Mateo turned back to the door. Taking a deep breath, he knocked.

Nothing but silence.

"Dad?" Mateo called. "Are you in there?" He knocked again, louder this time. "Dad?"

There was still no answer.

Mateo tentatively pushed open the door, poking his head inside. "Dad?"

The office was empty.

Mateo's shoulders slumped, whether from relief or disappointment Margot wasn't sure. He swung the door the rest of the way open. "What are we supposed to do now?"

"Maybe he's at a meeting," Margot said. She stepped inside the office, nodding for Mateo to follow. "Let's see if we can find his schedule."

She led the way around Rodrigo's polished desk, noting with approval the neatly organized stacks of file folders and large supply of multicolored highlighters.

Margot loved highlighters.

Especially the orange ones.

"You check the computer," she instructed Mateo. "I'll take the desk."

Mateo smacked his forehead, pointing toward the old-fashioned office phone sitting next to the computer. "Or I could just *call* him."

"Oh," Margot said. "Right."

As Mateo pulled out his cell, Margot picked up the framed photo sitting next to Rodrigo's keyboard. Mateo and his father smiled up at her in matching baseball caps, their arms flung around each other's shoulders.

The family resemblance was unmistakable, even down to the cowlicks in their dark hair.

They looked like a family from a catalogue, Margot found herself thinking. Or models, posing for the photo they used to sell the picture frame.

Maybe it was just that they looked happy together.

"He's not answering," Mateo said, hanging up in frustration. "He *always* answers."

Margot, who hadn't spoken with *her* father in over a month, replaced the picture frame on the desk with a loud clunk.

Mateo dropped into his father's chair, swiveling moodily back and forth.

As he twisted his chair to face her direction, Margot caught sight of something.

"What?" Mateo asked, pausing mid-swivel. "What is it?"

Margot cleared her throat. Raising a finger, she pointed to the patch of dark brown leather just above Mateo's ear.

It was smeared with yellowish goo.

CHAPTER 17

"HE'S STILL NOT ANSWERING," MATEO said, shaking his head. "I've sent him, like, seven texts. *And* left a voice mail."

Margot watched as Mateo paced nervously back and forth in front of his father's desk, anxiously checking his phone every few seconds.

The adrenaline that had been pumping through her veins all morning had finally trickled to a halt, leaving her exhausted.

She had no idea where Mateo's father was, and no idea how to find him. She was hungry, and worried, and the air-conditioning in the office was making her shiver.

She felt useless.

Margot didn't like feeling useless.

She stood up. "Come on," she told Mateo. "Let's go."

He looked up from his phone. "Go where?"

"I don't know," Margot said. "But we'll figure it out on the way. Positive visualization!"

Mateo's forehead wrinkled in confusion. "What?"

"Positive visualization," she repeated. "I do it before wrestling matches. You picture your desired result in your head, and then . . . You know what?" she asked, trailing off. "Let's just start walking and see where it takes us. I mean, it's not like West Cove is that big of a town. Your dad has got to be around here *somewhere*."

"Okay. Yeah." Mateo nodded, pushing himself up from his chair. "You're right," he said. "Let's go."

He followed Margot into the hallway, pausing in the doorway for just a moment to peer around the office one last time. A tiny part of him almost believed that his dad might spring out from some secret hiding place behind a chair, shouting, "Surprise!"

He didn't, of course.

Things rarely work out the way we want them to.

Mateo was just closing the office door behind him when a loud scream echoed through the hallway.

Margot's head snapped up.

She whipped around to look at Mateo.

"Did you hear that?" she demanded.

"Of *course* I heard it," Mateo said. "It was a *scream*."

Margot took a step closer to Mateo, peering anxiously around the hallway. "Where did it *come* from?" she said.

Mateo took a step closer to Margot. "I don't know," he said. "Maybe that way?" He nodded vaguely around the corner, back the way they had come.

They stared down the hallway, waiting to see if the sound would come again.

It did. But they still couldn't tell which direction it came from.

"What do we do?" Mateo asked wildly.

"I don't know!" Margot shot back. She chewed anxiously on her lip. "Do you think it's your dad?"

"Maybe?" he asked. "I don't know!" He fought the urge to charge forward and run away at the same time, giving a weird little hop in place.

"Well, what does your dad sound like when he screams?" Margot demanded.

Mateo stared at her. "Are you kidding me?" he asked. "I don't know! Do *you* know what *your* dad sounds like when he screams?"

Years of wrestling practices flashed through Margot's head.

The unmistakable thud of a door being closed floated around the corner, distracting her.

Margot reached out, grabbing Mateo's arm.

High heels tapped against the wooden floor. High heels that were coming toward them.

Margot squeezed Mateo's arm.

"What do we do?" he mouthed, his eyes wide with fear.

Margot made a split-second decision.

"Hide," she mouthed back.

CHAPTER 18

"EXCUSE ME?" A VOICE CALLED out from behind them in a pleasant, yet firm, tone. "Children? Can I help you with something?"

Crouched behind an end table, Margot and Mateo stiffened. Margot slowly raised one finger to her lips, urging Mateo to be silent.

He nodded, his eyes wide.

"Hello?" the voice called out again, more insistently this time. "Children? I can see you, you know. Quite well, in fact."

Mateo looked at Margot. "Just . . . act normal," she whispered. "And be ready to run."

She closed her eyes, counting in her head. One. Two.

Before she reached the number three, she pulled herself to her feet.

An older woman with frosted blond hair was standing at the end of the hallway, her enormous pearl earrings gleaming in the overhead light. She was wearing a white silk blouse and a politely confused expression.

Beneath the layers of expensive makeup she wore, the woman's skin was sallow and sweaty. Dark circles ringed her eyes, and her lips looked chapped.

Next to Margot, Mateo reluctantly straightened. "Mayor Balboa?" he asked in surprise.

Leslie Balboa had worked with Mateo's father at city hall for over a decade. They were friends, as well as coworkers, and frequently attended each other's Christmas parties and barbecues. They also played together on the interoffice league bowling team, the Pin Pushers. They had matching bowling shirts and everything.

It was embarrassing.

"Mateo?" Mayor Balboa asked, drawing her eyebrows together. "Are you okay? What are you doing hiding in the hallway?" She sounded hoarse, as if she badly needed a drink of water.

"We were looking for my dad," Mateo said. "And then we heard—"

"Screams," Margot interrupted, giving Mayor

Balboa a speculative look. "We heard screams. Just now. You didn't?"

"Screams?" Mayor Balboa arched a well-manicured eyebrow. "Really?"

Mateo nodded. "Two," he said. "You didn't hear them?"

"Shouldn't you both be in school right now?" the mayor asked, neatly sidestepping Mateo's question.

"Have you seen Mateo's father?" Margot asked, neatly sidestepping the *mayor*'s question. "We need to find him. It's an emergency."

"An emergency?" Mayor Balboa. "What kind of an emergency?"

"A . . . bad . . . one?" Mateo asked.

From around the corner came a loud *thump*. Margot and Mateo jumped, Mateo's knee nearly knocking over the end table.

As he steadied himself against the wall, Margot narrowed her eyes, staring at the mayor.

The mayor narrowed *her* eyes, staring back at Margot.

"What was that?" Margot asked.

"What was what?" the mayor asked innocently.

Another *thump* echoed down the hallway.

"That," Margot said pointedly.

Mayor Balboa gave a delicate shrug. "I didn't hear anything."

The next *thump* was so loud it literally rattled the picture frames against their walls.

"You're one of them, aren't you?" Margot demanded.

The mayor smiled a cool, superior smile. "One of what, dear?"

"Wait, she's infected?" Mateo asked Margot. He turned to Mayor Balboa "You're *infected*?"

"Of course she's infected," Margot said. "Look at her. She looks terrible." The mayor bristled angrily, drawing her shoulders back. "Besides," Margot continued, "you said she was part of your dad's conservation club, right? Like Coach Jenkins?"

"Oh." Mateo swallowed. "Right."

The mayor's head jerked involuntarily to the side. She reached up to smooth the collar of her silk shirt, giving Margot and Mateo an appraising look.

Mateo elbowed Margot in the side. "I say we run for it," he whispered.

"Who was it that we heard screaming?" Margot demanded from the mayor. "What did you do to them?"

The mayor's lip curled back in a snarl.

"Um." Mateo took a step back. "Maybe we should

not make the alien angry? Let's just go," he urged.

The mayor sneered. "Yes. Why don't you children just . . . run along now?"

Margot lifted her chin. "Nice try," she said, stepping out from behind the end table. "But we're not going anywhere."

"Wait, *why* aren't we going anywhere?" Mateo asked. He pulled at Margot's arm, trying to tug her back. "We need *help*."

Margot planted her feet against the floor, making the most of her low center of gravity.

"What we need are answers," she said, glaring at the mayor. "Besides, I don't like being treated like a kid."

"You *are* a kid," Mateo pointed out. "We both are."

A soft growl escaped the mayor's lips.

"Fine," Margot said, not taking her eyes off the mayor. "Then go."

"I can't just leave you," Mateo protested.

Margot bent her knees, bracing for impact.

With an animalistic snarl, Mayor Balboa attacked. Her heels clattered against the wooden floor like machine gun fire as she flew across the hallway, her frosted blond head bent low.

"Aagh!" Mateo yelled, diving to the side.

Margot stood her ground.

As Mayor Balboa crashed into her, Margot's legs

shot out in a classic sprawl position. Rather than trying to fight the mayor's momentum, Margot continued to slide her legs back, pushing the weight of her hips down on the mayor's back. Pressing the mayor's neck into the floor with one hand, Margot used her other to block the mayor's arm. She spun around on top of the mayor, pulling the older woman into a headlock.

Mateo stared at her. "Whoa."

"Rope," Margot said through gritted teeth. The mayor was struggling with everything she had, including her teeth.

"What?" Mateo asked.

"*Rope*," Margot said again, forcing the mayor's chin up and away from her arm. "We need something to tie · her up with."

"Right. Okay," Mateo said. "Give me a sec."

He darted down the hall, back into his father's empty office.

"*Stop* it!" Margot told the mayor, who was still nipping angrily at Margot's arm. She tightened her grip around the older woman's neck, doing her best to ignore the goo-covered alien squirming beneath the mayor's collar.

It wasn't easy.

Mayor Balboa gave an angry shriek, drumming her heels against the floor.

"Will this work?" Mateo asked, racing back into the hallway. He triumphantly held a backpack up in front of Margot.

"I don't know," Margot said. "What's in it?"

"Oh. Right. Sorry," Mateo said. "It's my dad's rock climbing stuff."

Trying not to look at the mayor, he set the backpack on the ground and unzipped it. He rummaged around for a second, pulling a pair of shoes and several carabiners out. Finally, he pulled out a length of coiled rope.

"Perfect," Margot nodded. "Start with her feet."

"Um . . ." Mateo glanced uneasily at Mayor Balboa. "Okay, yeah," he said. "Sorry about this, Mayor. It's nothing personal, I swear."

Margot, who took being attacked *slightly* personally, rolled her eyes.

Mateo paused, twisting the length of rope nervously in his hands. He leaned closer to the mayor, lowering his voice. "Uh, do you think maybe you could not tell my dad about this?"

Mayor Balboa snarled in response.

Scooting quickly back, Mateo took the end of the rope and begin to wrap it around the mayor's feet. Soft Muzak continued to drone overhead as he worked quickly, looping the rope over itself then passing the end through front to back. Tightening the knot, he sat back on his heels.

"Done."

Margot glanced back over her shoulder. "Are you sure it'll hold?"

"Of course I'm sure," Mateo said, insulted. "Look at this thing. It's a textbook figure eight."

Margot blinked at him.

"It's, like, the most basic climber's knot there is," Mateo added. "What, have you never been climbing before?"

"I'm from *Iowa*," Margot pointed out. "How many cliffs do you think we have?"

Mateo shrugged. "Touchy, much?" he muttered, just loud enough to be heard.

She rolled her eyes. "Just come tie her hands, will you? I don't want her to get—"

She broke off as the mayor passed out cold, her head thudding loudly against the wooden floor.

CHAPTER 19

"WHICH ONE IS HER OFFICE?" Margot asked, trotting quickly down the hallway.

Mateo looped the rope one last time around the mayor's wrists, giving it a final tug to make sure it was secure. "It's on the left," he called, scrambling to his feet. "But wait for me! Sorry," he told Mayor Balboa, who had come to as soon as Margot had emptied an entire vase full of water over her head. "We'll get that thing off you as soon as we get back. You'll feel better soon, I promise."

The mayor spat on the floor in response.

Mateo took off, catching up with Margot just outside the mayor's door. She was already turning the handle.

"Hey!" he said. "Wait!"

Margot sighed, turning to face him. "Look, I get it, okay? If you want to wait out here, it's fine. But *I'm* going in."

Mateo straightened his shoulders. "I was going to say if anyone's going in first, it's going to be me." He pushed his sunglasses up, giving her a challenging look. "It's *my* dad who's missing, right?"

Margot blinked. "Right," she said, stepping to the side. "Be my guest."

Mateo nodded. "Okay. Yeah." He reached for the door handle. Closing his eyes, he summoned his courage.

"Are you doing the positive visualization thing I told you about?" Margot asked.

Mateo opened one eye, shooting her an annoyed look. "No!" he said. "Just give me a second, okay?"

"Okay." Margot lapsed into silence, impatiently tapping her sneaker against the floor.

Mateo closed his eyes again, steeling himself for whatever lay behind the door.

"Do you want me to count to three?" Margot asked helpfully. "I could, if you want me to. I don't mind."

Mateo opened both eyes. "It's fine," he said through gritted teeth. "Let's just do this."

And, before his brain could catch up with his body,

he twisted open the door handle. Pushing his way inside the office, he spun wildly around, searching for the source of the screams. "Dad?" he called. "Are you in here? *Dad?*"

Silence.

Mateo's entire body sagged with disappointment.

Next to him, Margot turned cautiously back and forth, her eyes sweeping quickly over the mayor's furniture.

It was considerably nicer than the furniture in Mateo's father's office.

"Helphhh!"

Mateo's and Margot's heads whipped automatically toward the sound of the muffled cry.

"Hellllphhhh!" the voice came again, louder this time.

Oddly enough, the cry appeared to be coming from the wood-paneled wall behind the mayor's desk.

Margot squinted in confusion. "Where's it coming from?" she asked.

Mateo raced around the mayor's desk. With a practiced shove, he pushed on the edge of one of the wood-paneled sections.

A hidden door swung open to reveal the mayor's private bathroom.

Chelsea Mandetti sat duct-taped to the toilet, a silk

scarf (probably the mayor's) knotted around her mouth.

"Huh," Margot said, tilting her head curiously to the side. "I was *not* expecting that."

"Oww!" Chelsea yelled. She massaged her reddened wrists, glaring up at Margot from her seat on the toilet.

"Sorry. But there's really no good way to remove duct tape," Margot said matter-of-factly.

"You didn't even try!" Chelsea said. "You just ripped it off!"

"Can we focus?" Mateo asked, hovering in the doorway. "What are you doing here, Chelsea?"

"What do you think?" she asked, shooting a final glare in Margot's direction. "I followed you guys."

"What about Calvin?" Margot asked. "You just left him alone? Unconscious? With an alien?"

"Uh-uh," Chelsea shook her head. "No way. You don't get to make this seem like it's *my* fault. *You guys* are the ones who left him in that closet. Besides," she said, shrugging, "you left a note for him."

Margot ripped the duct tape from around Chelsea's ankles with a loud *frriiip.*

"Ouch!" Chelsea screamed. "Stop that!"

Margot held up her hands in surrender. "That was the last piece. I swear."

"So what happened? I mean, why did Mayor Balboa

tape you up in here?" Mateo asked.

"She didn't infect you, did she?" Margot asked. Craning her neck, she peered over Chelsea's shoulder. "Do you mind lifting your hair again?"

"Yes, I mind," Chelsea said, swatting Margot's hand away. "I'm fine, okay? The mayor didn't *do* anything to me. She found me in the hallway, looking for you. She said she was going to report me for truancy, so I told her I was just following you guys. When she found out you were looking for Mateo's dad, she just got all weird and snarly, and then she locked me in here!"

"That was your mistake," Margot said, nodding. "The aliens are controlling their hosts' bodies. They only attack when they feel threatened."

Chelsea stared at her. "Are you serious?" she asked.

"Usually," Margot said.

Chelsea turned purposefully away from Margot. "So this is for real," she said. "Aliens. They're *really* real?"

Mateo nodded. "Yeah."

Out of the corner of her eye, Margot spied something through the bathroom window. Stepping up to the small square of frosted glass, she pressed her nose against the pane.

"For real," Chelsea confirmed. *"Actual real aliens."*

Mateo nodded again. "Pretty much."

Chelsea exhaled. "Okay," she said, thinking aloud.

"So, if like, aliens are real, then . . . what do they want?"

"Mateo," Margot interrupted. "Do you know what kind of car the mayor drives?"

"A black BMW," he said promptly. "Seven Series. Why?"

"I'm not sure what the aliens want," Margot said. "But whatever it is, it has something to do with salt. A *lot* of it."

She pointed out the window in explanation. Chelsea and Mateo crowded around, peering through the glass.

Just outside, Mayor Balboa's BMW was clearly visible in the city hall's parking lot. The lid of the trunk was suspended in midair, the back of the car stuffed with giant, yellow bags of rock salt.

"Coach Jenkins was carrying salt, too," Mateo said. "Remember? They must be taking it somewhere. A meeting point or something. I bet that's where my dad is!"

Margot nodded. "But *where*?"

Mateo pushed back his sunglasses, his expression determined. "I don't know," he said. "But I can think of someone who does."

CHAPTER 20

"LOOK." MATEO FOLDED HIS ARMS across his chest, staring menacingly down at the mayor. "We can do this the easy way, or we can do this the hard way. It's up to you."

Standing next to him, Margot tilted her head curiously to the side. "What's the hard way?" she asked Mateo, interested.

On the other side of Mateo, Chelsea poked her head forward. "Uh, for the record, none of this was my idea." She turned to the mayor, over enunciating her words to be on the safe side. "*None* of it."

Mateo shot both Margot and Chelsea an irritated look. "Just let me do this, okay? I've got, like, a thing going on here."

Margot looked dubious. "I just don't think it's working as well as you think it is. I mean, she doesn't even look scared."

She gestured down at Mayor Balboa, who was glaring up at them with what can only be described as "icy fury." A piece of duct tape, taken from the same roll she had used to restrain Chelsea, was pressed over her mouth.

It was the only way the children could stop the mayor from trying to bite them.

"I think you're just making her *more* angry," Chelsea commented.

"Chelsea's right. I don't think she's going to talk as long as that thing's attached to her back," Margot said. "We should just pull it off."

"That's what . . . I was *going* to . . ." Mateo gave up. "Fine," he said, uncrossing his arms. "We'll just pull it off. Happy?"

Margot rolled her eyes. "Chelsea, can you look for something to put the alien in, after we remove it? Some sort of container? Something with a lid, obviously."

"Fine. But just so you know, I am *not* touching that thing," Chelsea warned, heading off to look for a container.

"Go ahead," Margot told Mateo, gesturing toward the mayor. "I'll help hold her."

"Er . . ." Mateo looked awkwardly down at Mayor

Balboa. "Are you sure I should be the one to . . . Because *you've* done it bef—" He cut off abruptly at the sight of Margot's expression. "I mean, I'll do it. Obviously. I can do it."

Kneeling beside the mayor, he gingerly reached out one hand.

The mayor growled loudly through her duct tape, struggling against her restraints.

Mateo's figure eight knots held tight.

Exhausted from her brief struggle, the mayor slumped back into a sitting position, looking sulkily up at Margot. The bags underneath her eyes were even more noticeable from this angle.

Margot nodded to Mateo. "Go ahead."

Mateo sucked in a giant breath. Reaching out quickly, he clamped his hand around the slimy creature just below the mayor's silk collar.

"It's *cold*," he said, revolted.

Margot arched her eyebrows. "I remember."

Shuddering in disgust, Mateo tightened his hold on the alien. He began to pull, the alien's glowing body stretching thinner and thinner as he yanked upward on it.

"It's not coming off," he grunted.

"You have to pull hard," Margot told him. "*Really* hard."

"What does it look like I'm doing?" Mateo panted, shooting her a quick glare. "It's, like, stuck or something."

"Here," Margot said. "Let me do it."

Mateo let go of the alien. It snapped back against the mayor's neck, spattering thick drops of yellow mucus everywhere.

"Sick," Mateo breathed, staring down at his T-shirt.

Mayor Balboa let out a particularly loud growl, mumbling something unintelligible beneath her duct tape.

Margot wasn't sure, but she thought she could make out the words "you'll pay" and "dry cleaning."

Brushing a splotch of yellow goo from the front of her hoodie, she took Mateo's place on the floor. Steeling herself, she reached out and gripped the alien. It was somehow even more disgusting than she'd remembered.

"Watch and learn," she told Mateo. Leaning backward, she yanked at the alien with everything she had.

It didn't work.

Margot dug deep. Standing up, she closed her other hand around the alien as well, straining backward.

Nothing.

"See?" Mateo said. "I *told* you."

Margot let go of the alien, wiping her hands on her jeans. She bent low, examining the creature up close. "Look at this," she told Mateo, pointing down at the mayor's neck. "You see the little tentacle thingies? It looks like they're going *into* her neck." She shook her head. "Yours wasn't like this."

She bit her lip, staring down at the alien. "This is bad, Mateo. I don't think we should try to pull it out. What if the tentacles are wrapped around her spine or something? We could *paralyze* her."

Mateo slumped against the wall. "So how are we supposed to find my dad?" he asked.

Margot shook her head. "I don't know," she said softly. "I'm so sorry, Mateo."

She hesitated for a moment.

Then, screwing up her courage, she reached out and took Mateo's hand in hers.

She waited to see if he would pull away.

When he didn't, she gave a gentle squeeze.

Mateo didn't look at her.

But a second later, she felt him squeeze back.

"Jackpot!" Chelsea turned the corner, brandishing a Tupperware container triumphantly in front of her. "I had to rinse out this completely disgusting casserole thing. It was, like, *furry*, so you guys owe . . ."

She trailed off as she saw Margot's and Mateo's expressions.

Chelsea lowered the Tupperware. "What's wrong?"

CHAPTER 21

"SO TELL ME AGAIN WHY we can't just go to the police?" Chelsea asked. With one hand, she cupped her fingers over her nose, attempting to block out the stench of dead whale. With her other hand, she held the back door open for Margot and Mateo.

"Because I realized the chief of police is in the same conservation club as my dad," Mateo said, narrowly avoiding bashing the mayor's head against the door frame as he made his way through to the parking lot.

"Okay," Chelsea said. "So what?"

"So the mayor is part of the club. Coach Jenkins is, too. Which means if the chief is a member, too, he's probably already infected as well," Margot said through her surgical mask, following Mateo through the door. "Which means the rest of the police might be infected, too."

"Awesome," Chelsea said flatly. "That's just . . . awesome." She let the door swing shut behind Margot, looking around the parking lot. "So . . . what's the plan?"

Margot and Mateo looked at each other.

Chelsea closed her eyes for a second. "Please tell me you guys have a plan. Or are you just carrying the mayor around for fun?"

Mateo looked down at the mayor. She blinked listlessly up at him, all of the fight gone out of her. Her skin looked clammier than before, now that they were outdoors.

Mateo gave her as reassuring a smile as he could manage. "Don't worry," he said. "We're not just going to leave you here."

"We *do* have a plan, right?" he asked, turning to Margot.

"Right," she said confidently. "I mean, yes. Kind of."

Mateo and Chelsea waited expectantly for her to continue.

"It's still in the early stages," Margot said. "Less of a plan and more of an . . . idea. But I think this is a good step one," she added. "Definitely."

"Can you take that mask off?" Chelsea asked. "Your voice is all weird and muffle-y. Plus, you look ridiculous."

"I'm pretty sure me looking ridiculous is the least of our problems right now," Margot said. "We need to figure out what we're going to do."

"I thought you said you had a plan," Chelsea said.

"I said an *idea*," Margot stressed. "An idea is different from a plan."

"Whatever it is, can it maybe involve putting the mayor down for a second?" Mateo asked. "Because she's getting really heavy."

Margot nodded, glancing around to make sure no one was watching them. The back of city hall shared a parking lot with the West Cove Recreational Center. Thankfully, it was only open on weekends during the off-season.

"Here," she said, nodding toward the wooden bench beside the door. "Put her on this."

Working together, they laid Mayor Balboa down as gently as possible. Her eyelids fluttered up and down a few times before closing.

"Is she asleep?" Mateo asked, rolling his neck back and forth to loosen his muscles. "Or did she pass out again?"

"She doesn't look so good," Chelsea observed, still

covering her nose. "Are you sure you didn't, like, do something to her?"

"She was out for ten seconds, max," Margot said. She leaned closer, examining the mayor's cracked, swollen lips. "Whatever's happening to her, it has nothing to do with me accidentally . . . it has nothing to do with me."

"Shouldn't we get her to a hospital?" Mateo asked uneasily. "I mean, I know she, like, attacked you, and taped you up or whatever, Chelsea, but she's not normally like that, I swear. She's really nice. Well," he amended. "I mean, she's kind of scary if you don't know her. But she means well. And she never forgets my birthday."

Margot sat down on the sidewalk next to the bench and pulled out her phone.

"What are you doing?" Mateo asked.

"I thought maybe that lifeguard guy would have written back," she said. "Remember? I emailed him. But there's nothing."

"What lifeguard guy?" Chelsea asked in confusion. "Why don't I know about a lifeguard guy?"

"It doesn't matter," Margot said, shoving her phone back in her pocket. "He's not answering."

"We can't just do nothing," Mateo said. "We need a plan!"

"Well, *you* come up with one then," Margot shot back

at him. "Why am I the one who always needs to think of everything?"

"Guys," Chelsea said.

"Are you kidding me?" Mateo scoffed. "You love telling people what to do."

"And you love being *told* what to do," Margot said, crossing her arms against her chest and glaring up at him.

Something in the air shifted around them.

"What does that even mean?" Mateo asked.

"It means you're completely desperate for people to like you," Margot said. "It's so obvious. I heard Todd in the hallway earlier, talking about that game you lent him. He didn't even *care* that his dog ruined it. He's just taking advantage of you!"

Mateo glared back at her. "Oh, yeah? Well, excuse me if I'd rather have people like me than be some loner *weirdo*."

Margot flinched.

"Guys, there's a *van*—" Chelsea said, pointing.

"You know why everyone thinks you're so good in the play?" Margot asked Mateo. "It's because you're used to it. *Everything you do* is an act. I mean, your precious polo shirts? You literally wear a *costume* every day, just so that people will think you're interesting."

"What about you?" Mateo asked. "The *big, important*

wrestling star who's too stuck-up to even talk to anyone. I bet you think you're too cool for everyone. But the truth is no one can stand to be *around* you."

"Oh, yeah?" Margot yelled. "Well, at least I don't wear sunglasses *inside*!"

"You guys!" Chelsea waved her hands in front of her, stamping her feet to get their attention. *"Van."*

With a final glare at each other, Margot and Mateo turned to look at the boxy white van that was just turning into the parking lot.

In the driver's seat sat Calvin Biggs.

CHAPTER 22

CALVIN PULLED TO A STOP at the curb, peering curiously out the driver's side window. "Do I want to know why the mayor of West Cove is tied up on a bench outside city hall?"

"It was their idea," Chelsea said, pointing at Margot and Mateo. "I had nothing to do with it, I swear."

Margot rolled her eyes. "Tattle much?"

Chelsea nodded toward the mayor. "You realize this is technically kidnapping, right? I mean, you get that?"

Margot turned back to Calvin. "How are you feeling?" she asked. "You don't have a concussion, do you? Because if you have a concussion, you shouldn't be driving."

"No, I don't have a concussion," Calvin said. "Although you'd already know that if you hadn't abandoned me in a middle school supply closet. Unconscious. With an *alien* two feet away from me."

"Sorry," Margot said. "You obviously got our note, though."

Calvin opened the door, stepping out onto the sidewalk. "Never mind," he said. "Just explain why we're here." He nodded toward the bench. "Maybe start with her."

"Have Margot explain it to you," Mateo said, striding off farther into the parking lot. "After all, she knows everything," he called over his shoulder.

"You're acting like a child," Margot called after him.

"I *am* a child," Mateo called back. "So that doesn't even count as a burn."

Chelsea sighed. "I'll go after him," she said. "Try not to take anyone else prisoner while we're gone."

Margot watched Chelsea head after Mateo with a curiously empty feeling in her stomach.

It was fine, she told herself.

After all, everything she'd said to Mateo was true. If he couldn't handle the truth about himself, that was his problem.

But as she turned to Calvin and began filling him in on what he'd missed, a tiny part of her brain couldn't

107

help turning the argument over and over in her head.

Everything she'd said about Mateo was true.

So what did that mean about everything he'd said about her?

"So that's it," Margot said, nodding at the mayor. "When you pulled up, we were trying to figure out if we should bring her to the hospital. We should, right? Something's clearly wrong with her. I mean, something more than aliens."

Calvin finished examining the mayor, sitting back on his heels. "Dehydration," he said briskly. "I'm not a medical doctor, but I know the signs. Fever, rapid heart rate, clammy skin. Look at her lips. And here." He gently pinched the mayor's cheek. "See how slowly the skin sinks back? It's dehydration."

"The salt," Margot said slowly. "Coach Jenkins was carrying salt, remember? And look, the mayor's trunk is *stuffed* with it. There's got to be a link, right? Maybe the aliens need salt to survive," she said excitedly. "But, like, a lot of it. So much that it's dehydrating their hosts."

"We need to get someplace where I can examine the alien specimens more closely," Calvin said. He stared thoughtfully at his NOAA van. "I should be able to put together some sort of banana bag IV drip to help with the mayor's dehydration," he said. "It's really just about optimizing the sodium and dextrose ratio, I think."

"If you say so," Margot said. "But where are we going to—"

"You guys!" Chelsea called from the parking lot, waving at them. "Mateo has a plan! We need to go to his house."

Calvin shrugged. "Works for me," he said.

Margot hesitated. Then, lifting her chin, she forced herself to meet Mateo's gaze. "Fine," she said coolly. "Whatever."

"I wasn't asking your permission." Mateo scowled at her. He turned to Calvin. "How much room is there in that thing?" he asked, pointing toward the van. "We need to load all of this, too." He tapped the bags of salt in the mayor's trunk.

"*All* of it?" Calvin asked. "Why?"

Mateo flicked his sunglasses down onto his nose, staring purposefully at Margot as he did. "Bait," he said. "It's going to be bait."

CHAPTER 23

MATEO'S HOUSE WAS DIFFERENT THAN Margot had expected.

In her head, she had pictured something cool and modern. Stainless-steel appliances, maybe. Black leather sofas. A television that took up an entire wall.

She hadn't pictured flower beds. Or old-fashioned wallpaper on the walls. Or . . .

"Is that a pink refrigerator?" she asked, pointing at the kitchen. Mateo picked up an overstuffed needle-point pillow from the couch and walked over to the dining room table, gently sliding it beneath the mayor's head.

"Yeah," he said shortly, not meeting Margot's eye. "It is."

"It's cool," Margot said. "I didn't know they made pink fridges."

"Yeah? Well, I guess you don't know everything after all."

Margot felt a tiny stab of . . . something . . . in her stomach.

"Um, listen," she said, feeling unaccustomedly awkward. "I'm sorry, okay? About what happened before. I didn't mean to . . . I mean, I *meant* it, but I didn't mean . . . I wasn't . . ." She trailed off.

"Just forget about it, okay?" Mateo said. "It's not a big deal."

"If you say so." Margot plucked at her ponytail. "I guess we have bigger stuff to worry about right now," she said, still feeling uneasy about their fight.

"Do you have a coatrack?" Calvin asked, gingerly setting the glass aquarium on the card table Mateo had set up for him. Chelsea followed him reluctantly through the door, carrying a cardboard box full of supplies. "We need something we can hang the banana bag from. When it comes to intravenous fluids, gravity is our friend."

"Yeah," Mateo said. "One sec." He looked down at his wrinkled T-shirt, which was now covered in dried blotches of alien goo. "I'm going to grab another shirt, too. Anyone else need anything?" he asked, heading for the stairs. "If you're hungry, there's sandwich stuff in the fridge," he called over his shoulder. "Just help yourself."

Margot's stomach rumbled in response.

It was almost noon, and fighting aliens burned a lot of calories.

As Calvin busied himself with unpacking supplies on the dining room table, Chelsea and Margot wandered into the kitchen.

It was like something out of a movie set, Margot found herself thinking. The floor was covered in old-fashioned, huge black-and-white squares of linoleum, and the kitchen table was straight out of the fifties. Even the toaster looked retro, with round edges and bubble-gum-pink sides that perfectly matched the fridge.

"Mateo and his dad are really into old stuff, huh?" Margot asked, trying to figure out how the latch on the refrigerator door opened.

Chelsea stepped forward, motioning for Margot to move over. "Not really," she said. She lifted the latch easily, swinging the door open and looking inside. "Mateo's mom was, though. I don't think they've changed much since she died." She wrinkled her nose, lifting a bottle of mustard to examine it in the light. "Including their condiments, apparently."

Margot fiddled with the end of her ponytail,

watching as Chelsea rummaged through the bottom drawer. "You were friends with Mateo back then?" Margot asked. "I mean, before his mom . . . you know."

"Died?" Chelsea asked, arching an eyebrow at Margot. "Yeah. I mean, everyone here knows everyone else. Well, except for you, I guess." She held up a plastic bag full of sandwich meat. "Are you good with ham?"

Margot nodded absently.

"Cool," Chelsea said. "Do you want to check the cupboard? See if there's chips or anything? I could eat a horse right now."

As Chelsea busied herself with examining packages of cheese for mold, Margot drifted over to the shiny, white-painted cabinets. A photo tucked into the corner of the woodwork caught her eye, and she paused to look at it.

She recognized Rodrigo from the photo in his office, although he looked younger in this picture. There was also a patchy mustache creeping across his upper lip, Margot noticed. A much younger Mateo sat in Rodrigo's lap, probably seven or eight at the most. Mateo was grinning, his curly hair corkscrewing all over the place, his tongue sticking out at the camera.

Next to them sat a laughing woman, pretty, but with cheeks that looked just a little bit too thin somehow. She wore bright red lipstick and an oversize white button-down. A pair of vintage, gold-rimmed sun-glasses were perched on top of her head.

Margot leaned closer, staring at the sunglasses.

Her stomach clenched in regret as she recognized them.

They were the same ones that Mateo never took off.

CHAPTER 24

"ARE YOU SURE I CAN'T help?" Margot asked. "I know I broke a slide, but—"

"*Two* slides," Chelsea said, carefully handing Calvin a glass cover slip to position on top of the slide he had just set up. "You broke *two* slides. Snapped them like the Hulk."

"Can I help it if I'm strong?" Margot retorted. "I've got a lot of adrenaline running through me right now!"

Calvin slid the freshly prepared slide beneath the microscope he'd set up on a card table in the corner.

Margot glared at Chelsea.

Chelsea shrugged. "Sorry," she said insincerely.

"This is fascinating," Calvin said, not lifting his head

from the microscope. "The specimen Margot removed from Mateo's back appears to be vastly different from the one currently attached to the mayor. Almost as though there are different stages in the life cycle."

"What, like a tadpole turning into a frog?" Chelsea asked.

Margot, who had been about to ask the same thing, glared at Chelsea a little bit harder.

"What?" Chelsea asked in annoyance. "You're not the only one who can know things about stuff." She turned back to Calvin. "I'm right, aren't I?"

Calvin nodded. "Exactly right. In the 'tadpole' stage, the alien entities are still in a sort of stasis. They can't *grow*, but they *replicate* themselves. Classic asexual reproduction," he said gleefully. "Then, once they attach to a host, they're able to draw the necessary nutrients from its body, kick-starting their growth. The 'frog' stage, if you will."

"Uh-huh," Margot said. "So have you figured out how to get the 'frog' off the mayor yet?"

"Oh, er, not yet," Calvin said, dropping his eyes to the microscope again. "Although my banana bag seems to be working nicely," he added, gesturing vaguely toward the coatrack Mateo had dragged out of the hall closet for him. A Ziploc bag full of fluids hung suspended from it, a length of plastic tubing leading into the mayor's arm.

Mayor Balboa was still asleep, but her cheeks looked fuller, and her color had drastically improved.

"Great. But maybe focus on the part where we stop the aliens from draining everyone's body fluids and, you know . . . killing them?" Margot suggested. "Just a thought."

Calvin nodded, not looking up. "Right. Good tip. Chelsea, can you start preparing another slide?"

"On it," Chelsea said, nudging her way past Margot to reach the box of glass strips. "Do you mind?"

"Sorry," Margot said, taking a step back. She hovered uncertainly next to Calvin's chair for a moment, feeling oddly useless.

It wasn't a feeling she enjoyed.

"I'm just going to see if Mateo's heard anything from his dad yet," she said. "But let me know if I can do anything."

Bending low over one of the slides, Chelsea gave her a careless wave. "Okay. Whatever."

Margot scowled. Pausing in front of the door, she pulled her mask from her pocket and started to slip it over her head. Then, thinking better of it, she stuffed it back into her pocket.

Opening the door, she braced herself against the smell of dead whale then stepped out.

"Hey," she said to Mateo, letting the door fall shut behind her. "Have you heard anything yet?"

He shook his head, staring down at his phone. "Nothing," he said. "I don't even think he's seen it yet."

He glanced up at the bags of salt they'd stacked temptingly in the front yard before snapping a photo of them and sending it to Rodrigo.

"Maybe he has," Margot said encouragingly. "He could be on his way here right now, without texting back first."

Mateo shrugged. "I guess."

Margot sat down next to him on the top of the concrete steps. There was an empty blue-painted flower planter next her elbow.

The sun dipped behind a cloud for a second and Margot shivered, pulling the sleeves of her hoodie down over her hands. Mateo had changed back into another polo shirt, she noticed. This one had blue-and-green stripes.

She tried not to stare at the sunglasses perched on his head.

"Calvin and Chelsea are making progress in there," she said. "I guess the aliens reproduce asexually? Calvin's really excited about it."

"Awesome," Mateo said flatly.

"And the mayor's looking better, too," Margot said.

Her voice sounded too chipper, even to her own ears. "So that's . . . good."

"It's been almost two hours. He's not coming, is he?" Mateo asked. His eyes darted quickly toward Margot's, then away.

"What?" Margot asked. "No, of course he is. I mean, look at all that salt," she said, gesturing toward the stack. "How could anyone with an alien attached to their back pass *that* up?"

"It was a stupid idea," Mateo said. "I mean, there's got to be a dozen places in town where you can get salt. He's probably loading up at the hardware store right now."

"It wasn't a stupid idea," Margot said firmly. "It was a *good* idea. It's going to work, Mateo. Okay? Your dad is going to be fine."

Mateo picked a tiny pebble loose from the concrete, twisting it back and forth in his fingers. "Yeah. Only he might not be."

"He *will.*"

Mateo turned his head, really meeting her gaze for the first time since their argument. "Things don't always work out the way you want them to," he said. "Trust me. I know."

Margot opened her mouth to argue then closed it.

Mateo was right.

Things didn't always work out the way you want them to.

Sometimes, they didn't work out at all.

"I might just sit out here for a while," she said. "With you. Is that okay?"

Mateo nodded.

"Okay," Margot said. She folded her arms around her knees, pulling them closer to her chest. Dropping her chin to her knees, she waited with Mateo.

It was only a few minutes before they heard the sound of a two-hundred-pound table crashing to the floor.

CHAPTER 25

MARGOT AND MATEO MADE IT through the door in a tangled confusion of legs and arms. By the time they reached the dining room, Calvin was already pulling himself up from the floor, wincing in pain.

"Are you okay?" Margot whirled frantically around. "Where's Chelsea? And the mayor? What *happened*?"

Calvin pressed a hand against the back of his head, gingerly searching for cuts. "I don't know," he said. "She attacked me!"

"The mayor?" Mateo asked. "But she was tied up! I did the knots myself!"

"Yeah, I, um, I might have untied her," Calvin admitted. "She was being so cooperative, and I needed to get a sample, and . . ." He flinched away from Margot's gaze. "Anyway, it wasn't her that attacked me. It was *Chelsea*."

"What?" Mateo said. "Why?"

Margot smacked her hand against her thigh. "She must have been infected after all. We didn't check her neck in the mayor's bathroom, not really. How could we have been so careless?"

"Why didn't she say something?" Mateo asked. "We could have pulled it off her! It was probably barely attached at that point."

"Maybe she didn't know," Margot said. "Or, I don't know. Maybe she didn't *want* to know." She held out a hand, helping Calvin to his feet. "Are you okay?" she asked. "What did she hit you with?"

"I don't know," Calvin said, leaning unsteadily against the wall. "Whatever it was, it was heavy." He held his hand out in front of him, checking for blood. "You know, I'm getting kind of sick of being hit in the head," he observed.

"Are you kidding me?" Mateo scooped something off the floor, holding it up for Calvin and Margot to see. "She used my *Xbox*?"

"Focus," Margot said to Mateo. Then, turning back to Calvin, she asked, "Did you see which way they went?"

"Out the back," Calvin said.

"Maybe we can still catch them," Mateo said, starting for the kitchen. The sound of tires squealing against the pavement made him pause.

"Did I mention the mayor took my keys?" Calvin asked weakly. "And the other alien specimen?"

Margot turned automatically toward the card table, where the aquarium had last been sitting. It was gone.

"Great," Mateo said. "This is just *great*. The mayor's gone. Chelsea's gone. My *dad* is gone. And the only proof that aliens even exist is gone, too!"

"At least you don't have multiple head injuries!" Calvin said, scowling at him. "And your van isn't stolen."

"Technically, I think the van belongs to the NOAA," Margot said, coming back from the kitchen. "Here," she told Calvin. She thrust a bag of frozen peas in his direction. "I couldn't find any ice packs. Did you know all your ice cube trays are empty?" she asked Mateo.

"Not the issue right now," Mateo snapped back at her.

Calvin gingerly pressed the bag of peas against the back of his head, wincing at the coldness. Inside his pocket, his phone vibrated. "Oh, great," he said, pulling it out with his left hand and checking the number. "It's my boss. Perfect timing," he said sarcastically.

He answered the phone. "Hello?"

Mateo set his cracked Xbox down on the bureau, giving it a sad look.

"Yes, sir, I know. I'm sorry about lunch," Calvin said, rolling his eyes. "I completely forgot about bringing something back for you." He adjusted the bag of peas against his head. "There's been . . . a lot going on."

He held the phone slightly away from his ear as Dr. Smalls replied. The older man's voice was loud enough for Margot and Mateo to hear through the phone.

"Yes, sir, I'm sorry that the Cozy Inn's pool area is closed for maintenance, but—" He cut off as Dr. Smalls began to speak again. For a moment, Calvin allowed himself to dream of the day his boss would finally retire. Then something Dr. Smalls said made him snap his head up in attention.

"*What* was that, sir? Wait a minute!" Dropping the bag of peas to the floor, he gestured frantically for Margot and Mateo to gather around him and then pressed the speaker button on his cell. "Could you repeat what you just said?" he asked eagerly.

"I *asked*," Dr. Smalls growled on the other end of the line, his voice thick with annoyance, "why am I even talking to you on the phone when *the van is clearly parked in the lot outside*?"

Margot's eyes widened in realization.

"Are you *avoiding* me, Biggs?" Dr. Smalls demanded.

"Of course not, sir," Calvin said, cutting him off. "We'll be there as soon as we can."

"Who's 'we'? Where are you? And what about lun—"

Calvin hung up the phone.

"The Cozy Inn?" Margot asked. "You think that's where the aliens are meeting?"

Mateo bounced up and down on the soles of his feet. "Why not?" he asked. "I mean, why else would the mayor go *there*? Besides, it's not like we have another plan."

Calvin nodded. "The only problem is how we're going to get there," he said. "I suppose we could walk . . ." he said dubiously.

Mateo's eyes traveled past him, to a pair of keys hanging on the hook next to the door. "I might have a way," he said. "Can you drive stick?"

CHAPTER 26

"SHIFT!" MATEO CRIED, CRINGING AS the convertible's gears ground loudly against one another. "Shift!"

Calvin bit down on his tongue in concentration, pushing the stick shift forward. The car jerked in response, narrowly missing a mailbox.

"Careful!" Mateo called, shielding his eyes with his fingers. "This car is, like, fifty years old. It's my dad's baby. He is *not* going to be happy if you scratch it!"

"I'm trying my best!" Calvin shouted back, lurching forward again and nearly stalling the car. "This isn't as easy as it looks, you know."

Margot scooted closer to the window, trying to make more room for Mateo in the middle. "I thought you said you could drive a stick?" she asked Calvin.

"*Knowing* how to do something and actually *doing* it are two different things," Calvin said. "Hold on!"

He took a corner wide, sending Margot and Mateo flying against the door. Margot gritted her teeth as the handle jabbed awkwardly into her side.

An electronic reader board flashed as they passed the West Cove bank. "It's almost three?" she asked in surprise. A panicky feeling that had nothing to do with aliens ran through her body. She drummed her fingers agitatedly against her knee. "I can't believe we skipped an entire day of school. Do you think they called my mom?"

"Seriously?" Mateo asked, wincing as Calvin shifted gears again. "That's what you're worried about right now? *Skipping school?*"

"Well, I'm sorry," Margot snapped. "But it goes on your permanent record!"

"Permanent records aren't even real," Mateo countered. "They're just, like, this thing people made up to scare kids into good behavior."

"Tell that to the college admission boards," Margot retorted.

"Hey!" Calvin said. "Can you two not fight right now? I'm trying to concentrate!" He swung wide around another corner, narrowly avoiding the curb.

He bumped into the Cozy Inn's parking lot, pulling the convertible up directly in front of the main doors. With a sigh of relief, he cut the car's engine.

"Just in case anyone asks in the future," Mateo said. "You *so* cannot drive stick."

Calvin shot him a disgruntled look, but didn't deny it.

"We're here now," Margot said. "That's the important part. And look." She pointed toward the side parking lot, where the unmistakable NOAA van was parked crookedly next to the curb. "Your boss was right. They're here."

Mateo scrambled up on his knees, ignoring the marks his shoes were very possibly making on the leather seat. "There," he said, jabbing his finger. "Look! It's my dad's car! He's here!" Too impatient to wait for Margot to open the door, he scrambled over her lap and hopped out the side of the car.

Racing across the parking lot, he skidded to a stop outside his father's Prius, cupping his hands against the glass. "He's not in here," he called back over his shoulder, his voice a mix of disappointment and relief. "I can see his phone, though. He must have left it."

"At least that explains why he never got back to you," Margot said, exiting the convertible in a slightly more traditional way. "Is there anything else?" she asked, crossing the parking lot. She cupped her hands next to

Mateo's, peering through the window as well.

"I don't know," Mateo said, looking through the back window for something that might resemble a clue. "Do a bunch of Twix wrappers count?" He pushed away from the car. "C'mon," he told Margot. "Let's go."

Calvin jogged up to Rodrigo's car as well, gazing suspiciously around the empty parking lot. "Wait. I know we're all excited, but I think we should make a plan before we go in guns blazing."

"You have a gun?" Mateo asked in surprise.

"Of course not," Calvin said. "It's a figure of speech."

"Right," Mateo said, bouncing up and down on his heels. "Okay. You're right. We need a plan."

"We should talk to my boss," Calvin said. "He may have noticed something suspicious. Or at least have some sort of idea how many people we're dealing with. Although don't get your hopes up," he warned Margot and Mateo. "Dr. Smalls is pretty much the worst."

Mateo slipped his sunglasses down onto his nose. "Whatever," he said. "Let's do this thing."

CHAPTER 27

DR. SMALLS'S DAY HAD NOT improved since Calvin had left that morning.

He had lost seventeen games of solitaire in a row. He'd been forced to make do with vending machine snacks for lunch. And, for no reason at all that he could think of, his foot had suddenly started to hurt.

Dr. Smalls was just typing "foot cancer" into Google when Calvin burst into the multipurpose lounge, trailed by two young children. One of the children was, in Dr. Smalls's opinion, extremely grubby-looking.

To be fair, even if Margot *hadn't* been splattered in dried alien goo, she still wouldn't have made a good impression on the doctor.

Dr. Smalls wasn't a fan of children in general.

"Sir!" Calvin said. "I have something to tell you. It's important."

Dr. Smalls leaned back in his chair. He raked his gaze suspiciously up and down over Margot and Mateo, much in the same way he had eyed the questionable muffin from earlier that morning.

"Why do you have children with you?" he asked. "And where the heck have you been all day? Do you know what I was forced to eat for lunch, Biggs? Triscuits. That's all this miserable hotel had to offer me. *Triscuits.*"

Dr. Smalls wasn't a fan of Triscuits, either.

"Er, sorry about that, sir," Calvin said. "But like I said on the phone, things have been happening. Serious things. *Very* serious things. This morning, at the middle school, I—"

"How'd the talk go?" Dr. Smalls interrupted. He propped his feet up on the table in front of him, nearly knocking his full soda onto his keyboard. "I'll bet they ran all over you." He shook his head. "That's what's wrong with your generation," he said, stabbing a finger in Margot and Mateo's direction. "No respect."

Margot and Mateo exchanged glances. Mateo shrugged.

"Anyway," Calvin said. "Back to what I was saying. I

was at the middle school, and I saw something . . . these kids . . . well." He licked his lips. "It's hard to know how to describe it, sir."

"Aliens," Margot said, helping Calvin out. "I'd say 'aliens' pretty much sums it up."

"About this big," Mateo added, holding up his hands. "Bright blue. Covered in goo. Actually . . ." He leaned over the desk, craning his neck to check the back collar of Dr. Smalls's shirt. "All good," he told Margot and Calvin.

Dr. Smalls blinked at him. "Do you mind taking your hands off my desk, son?"

"Sorry," Mateo said, taking a step back. "Just checking to make sure you weren't infected."

"I know how it sounds, sir," Calvin said. "Believe me. But you just have to trust me. I've seen the aliens. I've examined specimens, up close, under a microscope. The genetic makeup is like nothing I've seen before. Anywhere. *Ever.*"

"Uh-huh." Dr. Smalls swiveled in his chair in Calvin's direction. "So what you're saying is, you didn't bring me back any lunch."

Calvin balled his hands into fists and counted to three. It was a stress control tip he'd developed after working with Dr. Smalls for several years.

"They're here. In *this* hotel. Have you noticed

anything suspicious this afternoon? People coming and coming? Anything like that?"

"How *many* people?" Margot asked. "What were they doing? And what about the pool area? How long has it been closed?"

"What about this guy?" Mateo asked, whipping out his phone and pulling up a picture of his dad. He shoved it in Dr. Smalls's direction. "Did you notice him? Did he look okay?"

Dr. Smalls scratched his armpit. "So no food," he said to Calvin, completely ignoring Margot and Mateo. "That's what you're telling me? None at all?"

"Forget about lunch!" Margot shouted, banging on the desk with the palms of her hands like she'd seen people do in the movies. "We're talking about an alien invasion here!"

A small sigh escaped Dr. Smalls's lips. "I don't know what you think you're playing at, Biggs, but I can assure you this isn't funny."

"Please, sir. I'm begging you," Calvin said. "You have to believe me!"

Dr. Smalls scratched his other armpit. "That's the thing, Biggs. I don't." Pushing back his chair, he stood up. In all the excitement, he'd completely forgotten about his aching foot.

"Now," the doctor told Biggs, "I'm going to go get a

late lunch. By the time I get back, the two of you?"—he pointed in Margot and Mateo's direction—"will be gone. Understood?"

"But—" Margot started to say.

"But—" Mateo said at the same time.

"No buts," Dr. Smalls said firmly, cutting them off. "And you," he said, turning to Calvin. "You're a grown man. Stop horsing around and start *acting* like it."

Calvin drew himself up to his full height of five feet seven inches. "I know how this sounds. But aliens are real, doctor. They're *real*."

Dr. Smalls looked up at the ceiling, shaking his head in disgust.

"Get it together, Biggs," he barked, storming out of the multipurpose lounge. *"Get it together!"*

"Well," Margot observed as the door swung shut behind him. "That went . . . not great."

CHAPTER 28

THERE WAS SOMETHING VAGUELY UNSETTLING about the Cozy Inn's main hallway, with its loud floral wallpaper, threadbare carpet, and flickering overhead lights. The air was thick and humid, and the smell of chlorine grew stronger with every step.

Calvin led the way toward the pool area, pausing every few seconds to stop and listen for footsteps. He carried a large stapler in one hand, and wore a grim expression.

Margot and Mateo followed behind him, tiptoeing quietly. Mateo was armed with an old-fashioned rotary telephone. He wasn't exactly thrilled with his choice of weapon, but in the end it had come down to the phone or a small, rubber, potted plant.

Margot, who preferred to rely on herself, carried nothing.

"Hey," Mateo said, turning to her as they walked. "Thanks for coming with me, by the way," he said in a low voice.

Margot stared straight ahead. "No problem."

"No, I mean it," Mateo said. "I mean, you didn't have to, or anything, but you did. So . . . thanks."

Margot let herself glance quickly in his direction. "It's okay," she said. "Really."

Shifting the phone into the crook of his right arm, Mateo awkwardly stuck his left one out. "Friends?" he asked.

The corners of Margot's lips gave an almost imperceptible twitch. She hurriedly forced them back into a serious expression. "Okay," she told Mateo. "Friends." Reaching out, she gave his hand a quick, firm shake.

Mateo grinned. Turning back to look at Calvin just in time, he pulled up short before running into the scientist.

"Look at this," Calvin breathed, nodding toward the large window set into the wall just ahead of them. Through the glass, the pool area was clearly visible.

It was bustling with activity.

A dozen or so adults were gathered around the

edge of the pool, busily dumping containers of salt into the water. Despite the heat of the room, they were fully dressed in their regular, everyday work clothes, although a few of them had loosened their ties or rolled their pant legs up.

"That's Mary," Calvin said, pointing toward a middle-aged woman near the deep end of the pool. "I recognize her. She's the hotel manager. What are they doing with all of those boxes?"

He and Margot watched curiously as the older woman methodically assembled a heavy-duty cardboard box, setting the finished product on top of the growing pile next to her. A few feet away, a middle-aged man was fitting smaller Styrofoam boxes with lids, carefully testing each one before setting it aside.

"I don't know, but there's Coach Jenkins," Mateo said, pointing. "Why is he just standing there like that?"

Coach Jenkins had centered himself directly in front of the cedar door that led to the Cozy Inn's sauna. He stood in a classic security guard pose, with his arms folded across his chest.

The circles underneath his eyes had grown noticeably darker since this morning.

"He looks like he's standing guard," Margot said. "But why would anyone stand guard in front of a sauna?" she wondered.

A small chill ran down her spine. For the first time in her life, Margot wasn't sure if she really wanted to know the answer to a question.

"Where's my dad?" Mateo said urgently. He pushed himself up on his toes, pressing his nose against the glass. "Do you see—"

"Matty?"

At the sound of his father's voice, Mateo whirled so quickly he nearly tripped. "Dad!" he shouted.

Rodrigo stood at the end of the hallway nearest the exit, staggering under the weight of a giant bag of rock salt. Dropping the telephone he was carrying to the ground, Mateo rushed forward, almost knocking his father over with the force of his hug.

Margot looked away, sudden jealousy clawing at the back of her throat.

"Are you okay?" Mateo asked, drawing back to look closely at his father.

The bag of salt slipped from Rodrigo's grip, thudding loudly to the floor. He looked, if possible, worse than the mayor had looked outside of city hall. His eyes were sunken and dull, his skin waxy and loose. He could barely stand, but he still smiled cheerfully at Mateo. "What are you doing here?" he asked his son. "Shouldn't you be in school?' His eyes traveled past Mateo to look at Calvin. "Do I know you?" he asked, recognition plucking at the corner of his mind.

"Er, Calvin Biggs," Calvin said, giving Rodrigo an awkward wave. "We've met. I'm with the NOAA?"

"Of course, of course," Rodrigo said. "And who's your friend?" he asked Mateo, his gaze coming to rest on Margot.

"Margot Blumenthal," she said. "I'm new."

Rodrigo gave her a welcoming, if slightly blank smile. "Nice to meet you, Margot. Any friend of Mateo's . . ." He trailed off, staring into space for a minute. Mateo shot Margot a worried look.

His dad gave himself a shake. "Well, I should be going," Rodrigo said. "Lots to do, you know." He clapped his hand weakly over Mateo's shoulder. "But I'm certainly looking forward to your performance tonight," he said as heartily as he could manage. "I thought afterward we could celebrate. How's ice-cream cake sound?"

Mateo forced a sickly smile. "Great. But, Dad, don't you think you should sit down for a minute? You're not looking so . . . good."

Rodrigo gave his son a hollow-eyed stare. "Don't be silly, Matty. Just fighting off a little cold, is all."

"I really think we should go home," Mateo said insistently. "Or better yet, the hospital. You're . . . sick . . . Dad. You need help."

"Nonsense," Rodrigo said, swaying in place. "I've never felt—"

His eyes fluttered back in his head, and he fell heavily forward against his son.

"Dad?" Mateo cried, staggering under his weight. *"Dad?"*

Margot and Calvin rushed forward to help him. Between the three of them, they lowered Rodrigo clumsily to the ground.

"He's okay," Calvin said, quickly checking Rodrigo's pulse. "I mean, obviously not, like, *okay* okay, but he's still alive. We need to get him a banana bag. *Fast.*"

Margot tightened her ponytail. "Let's get him out of here," she said. "We can come back for Chelsea and the mayor once we know he's safe."

Calvin nodded. "Agreed."

Mateo gripped his father's hand, nodding rapidly up and down. "Okay. Yeah. Let's do it," he said.

"Lift on the count of three," Margot said. "One. Two."

"Three," said a sugary sweet voice behind them. Mayor Balboa stepped out from the side hallway, flanked on either side by a burly, sport-coated man.

Chelsea stood just behind the adults, a wide smirk on her face.

"Surprise," she said.

CHAPTER 29

"IT'S NO USE," MATEO SAID, watching Margot struggle against her restraints. "They're figure eight knots."

Margot wriggled harder.

"I feel like I'm getting rope burn just watching you," Mateo said. "Trust me, it's not going to work, okay? So you might as well just relax."

Margot threw back her head, letting out a frustrated scream.

Next to her, Calvin winced. "Do you mind?" he asked groggily. "Some of us have a headache here."

His head lolled to the side, his eyes flickering closed. A dark bruise was already blooming over his eye where the mayor had punched him. It almost perfectly matched the bruise from Coach Jenkins's earlier punch.

"Should we be worried about him?" Mateo asked. "He's been hit in the head *a lot* today."

Margot slumped back against the wall, momentarily giving up on the ropes. "You're right," she said grudgingly. "This isn't going to work. They're too tight."

Mateo resisted the urge to say *I told you so.*

He wasn't in the mood to gloat.

"Why aren't they doing anything for him?" he asked Margot. He gritted his teeth in anger, staring hard at his dad. A couple of the mayor's flunkies had carried him in from the hallway, laying him off to the side on a pile of tarps, then gone back to work.

"I mean, they're just going to let him *lie* there? Hey!" Mateo called out in a louder voice. "You, guy with the pool skimmer!" Mateo banged his hands against the floor, trying to get the attention of the worker. He thought he might vaguely recognize him from city hall, but couldn't remember his name. "I'm talking to you!" Mateo yelled.

A smiling man in a postal uniform upended a fifty-pound bag of rock salt into the shallow end of the pool. The man with the skimmer leaned forward, swishing it vigorously around to mix the salt in.

He appeared to be whistling while he worked.

"Postman guy!" Mateo yelled, giving up on the man

with the pool skimmer. "Hey, you! In the shorts! Talk to me!" Mateo pounded the floor again. "*Someone* talk to me!"

From the other side of the pool, Chelsea shot them a nasty look. "We've already told you to be quiet!" she called out. "Don't make me get the duct tape!"

Mateo glared at her. "Traitor!" he called out. "That thing attached to your back is going to kill you, you know that? It's going to kill *everyone*!"

Chelsea snarled at him. Ripping open a canister of kitchen salt in a particularly violent fashion, she upended it into the pool.

Mateo dropped his head back against the wall. "I can't believe this," he said. "Aliens. *Aliens.* We're all going to die, because of *aliens*. Like, is *this* how you pictured yourself going out?" he asked, gesturing around the pool area with his chin.

Margot tilted her head to the side, considering the question.

"Not really," she admitted.

She and Mateo lapsed into silence, watching the buzz of activity around them.

It was hot in the pool area. Beneath her hoodie, the armpits of her T-shirt were growing damp. The chlorine in the air was making her throat itch.

She was hungry, and thirsty, and tired, and scared.

She also needed to pee.

Staring at a large pool full of water wasn't helping.

Margot thumped up and down a few times, shifting her body so that she could look at Mateo instead. "Sorry about all of this," she said. "It really sucks. Especially about your dad. He seems nice."

"Yeah," Mateo said, looking pointedly at the wall above Margot's head. He blinked a few times, clearing his eyes. "He's pretty cool. You know, for a dad."

"You hang out together a lot, huh?"

"Yeah," Mateo said, shrugging. "I mean, you know. He's my dad."

"My dad and I never hung out," Margot said matter-of-factly. "Other than practice, I mean." She stared at the tips of her sneakers, choosing her words carefully. "I think he liked me more as a wrestler than a daughter."

"What?" Mateo asked. "That's ridiculous."

Margot didn't say anything.

"You *know* that's, like, ridiculous, right?" Mateo repeated. "Of course your dad likes you."

"You know what he said when I told him that I didn't want to wrestle anymore?" Margot asked quietly, still looking at her shoes. "He said that he 'wasn't going to have a quitter as a daughter.'"

"You're not going to wrestle anymore?" Mateo asked.

Margot gave him a look.

"Sorry," he said quickly. "I mean, that's not great, what your dad said, but I'm sure he didn't mean—"

"He stopped talking to me. It was like he couldn't even look at me anymore. And then Mom got a new job here, and we left. And he stayed." She cleared her throat. "He's not moving out here. Ever."

Mateo was silent.

Margot looked at Mateo. "Sorry," she said. "It's not your problem. I shouldn't have said anything."

"No." Mateo gave an awkward nod. "It's cool. I'm glad you did."

Next to Mateo, Calvin's head snapped up. He groaned, cracking his eyes open to squint against the light. "What's going on?" he croaked. "Did we win yet?"

"Uh, it's been, like, two minutes, dude," Mateo said. "Literally nothing's happened."

"Oh." Calvin closed his eyes again. "I kind of thought you'd have cut us free by now."

Margot rolled her eyes. "Cut us free with what?" she asked. "The mayor took everything. That stapler you had, our phones . . . I'm surprised she didn't take Mateo's sunglasses."

Mateo looked horrified at the thought.

Calvin blinked groggily. "Can't we just use my knife?"

CHAPTER 30

"WHAT KNIFE?" MARGOT DEMANDED, SITTING up straighter.

"My knife," Calvin said, nodding toward his leg. "The one I keep in my boot."

Margot and Mateo both stared at him.

"You keep a secret knife in your boot?" Mateo asked.

"It's not a *secret*," Calvin said. "I just keep one there. It comes in handy when you're out in the field." He gave a slightly woozy nod. "Not all science happens in a lab, you know."

"So why were you carrying a stapler then?" Margot asked curiously. "If you had a knife this whole time?"

Calvin blinked. "Oh. Yeah. I guess I forgot."

"All right, people, that's all of it!" a voice called out.

Mayor Balboa stood on the edge of the diving board, beaming out at the crowd. She was still pale, with giant circles under her eyes, but she'd somehow found the time to restyle her hair and change into a new blouse. "Let's give ourselves a round of applause for all of our hard work!"

The adults in the room broke into a cheer, raucously clapping their hands. The man with the pool skimmer waved it jauntily back and forth through the air like a flag.

Mayor Balboa held her hands out, urging everyone to quiet down.

"Although this swimming pool may seem a humble abode for such a mighty creature, rest assured this is only a temporary solution. Soon, her precious cargo will have been shipped to every corner of the world. The need for secrecy will be gone. Our Queen Mother will emerge, *triumphant!*"

Another cheer rose from the crowd. The mayor was an excellent public speaker.

"Uh . . ." Mateo whispered. "Did she just say, '*our Queen Mother*'?"

Margot turned to Calvin. "About this knife," she said.

Wordlessly, he swung his rope-bound legs around to face Margot and Mateo. "I can't reach," Margot said, straining forward. "Mateo, you're going to have to do it."

Mateo inched forward, edging a couple of fingers into Calvin's boot. "Sick," he groaned, wrinkling his nose. "It's all sweaty."

"*Deal with it*," Margot said.

Mateo grimaced, sticking his hand farther into the boot. A look of concentration crossed his face and he bit down on his tongue, wriggling his fingers back and forth.

Calvin let out a high-pitched laugh. "Sorry," he said, trying to compose himself. "It tickles."

Luckily, none of the infected people in the room seemed to hear him. Mayor Balboa silenced the crowd again. "And now, Coach Jenkins, if you're prepared to do the honors, I believe the time has come to welcome this magnificent creature to her new home!"

"Got it!" Mateo said triumphantly, pulling the small blade free.

Calvin stuck out his hands, nodding toward the length of rope that tied his hands together. "Be careful!" he said, wincing, as Mateo began to saw frantically back and forth with the knife.

"Slow is steady and steady is fast," Margot added.

"Will you shut up and just let me do it!" Mateo fired back at her. "It's harder than it looks, you know!"

"Stop distracting him!" Calvin said, wincing again as the knife slipped a little on the rope, narrowly avoiding his skin.

The crowd cheered louder than ever as Coach Jenkins nodded toward the mayor. Taking a step back, he placed his hand on the sauna door handle.

"First West Cove," the mayor called, pushing her hands dramatically toward the ceiling. "And, soon, the world!"

Coach Jenkins pulled open the door in one, quick motion.

Mateo's knife momentarily froze as he, Margot, and Calvin all turned to stare at the sauna in horror.

It was impossible to tell which one of them began to scream first.

CHAPTER 31

THE MASSIVE, GOO-COATED ALIEN LURCHED unsteadily out of the sauna, propelling itself forward on slime-covered tentacles.

It was huge, nearly twice as tall as Calvin; a disgusting, dripping, octopus-like creature with large, globby eyes and a wet, gaping mouth.

The Alien Queen made a thick, sucking sound as it turned its head back and forth, taking in its surroundings.

If it was surprised to find itself in the pool area of the Cozy Inn Hotel and Suites, it didn't show it.

"Isn't she beautiful?" Mayor Balboa cried delightedly, clasping her hands together in admiration. "Isn't she just the most wonderful creature you've ever seen?"

"I'm going to puke," Mateo moaned, looking ill.

"Pull yourself together," Margot said sharply. "Keep cutting."

Mateo swallowed hard, tearing his eyes away from the alien to look down at the ropes he was working on.

Calvin swallowed as well, his skin pale and sweaty. "Hurry up," he told Mateo in a high-pitched voice. "Hurry up, hurry up, *hurry up*."

The Alien Queen reared suddenly back, swiveling its huge, gelatinous head to look at the three of them. Its pale, filmy eyes stared beadily at them for a moment.

It gave a slow, deliberate blink.

Every adult in the room stiffened in response, whipping their heads to stare at Margot and the others. Mayor Balboa's lips curled back in a snarl.

"Crap," Mateo breathed. He sawed feverishly at Calvin's restraints. "Almost got it," he cried. "Almost got it . . . there!"

Calvin threw the ropes from his wrists. Grabbing the knife from Mateo, he sawed through the first rope still wrapped around his legs, then quickly unwound the rest.

Mayor Balboa jumped down from the diving board, striding deliberately toward the scientist.

"What did you *put* in that banana bag?" Mateo

cried. "She looks like the Terminator!"

"Here," Calvin shouted, tossing the knife to Mateo. "Cut each other free!"

He whirled to face the mayor, blanching a little at the sight of her.

Calvin licked his lips. "Um, ma'am, by order of the National Oceanic and Atmospheric Administration, I'm ordering you to stop. Right there. I mean it!"

Mayor Balboa smiled.

Launching herself forward, she tackled Calvin to the ground.

"Keep cutting," Margot said, thrusting her hands out in front of Mateo. She eyed the rest of the adults warily; they seemed to be frozen in place, waiting for instructions. "Come on. Hurry."

Mateo tore his gaze away from the alien. The disgusting, octopus-like alien was oozing unconcernedly toward the pool, its tentacles squelching against the tile.

Mateo bent his head low, focusing on Margot's restraints. "I'll tell you one thing," he muttered. "I'm never having calamari again."

Calvin had managed to haul himself to his feet again, shaking free from Mayor Balboa. "I'm not kidding," he panted. "This is serious!"

She aimed a side kick at his throat.

Mayor Balboa was a brown belt in karate; she liked

to stay active in her free time.

Calvin grunted, barely managing to dodge in time. "Stop it!" he shouted. "I'm including *all* of this in my report!"

Mayor Balboa swung her elbow horizontally at his jaw, connecting with a front elbow strike (this was not a traditional karate move; the mayor also dabbled in Muay Thai).

Calvin dropped to the floor again, momentarily stunned.

The mayor cracked her knuckles, staring down at him.

"There," Mateo said, slicing through the last strand of one of Margot's ropes. "Got it."

Margot untangled her hands, grabbing the knife from Mateo and starting on the ropes around her feet.

At the edge of the pool, the Alien Queen turned its dripping head to glance back at Margot. It paused, as if considering her. And then it blinked again.

Next to the sauna, Coach Jenkins snapped suddenly to attention. He turned slowly to face Margot and Mateo, his eyes narrowing.

He stepped forward.

CHAPTER 32

"CUT ME FREE!" MATEO YELLED.

"I'm still cutting *myself* free!" Margot yelled back.

On their right, Mayor Balboa had dropped to the ground on top of Calvin. Picking up his head, she slammed it against the tile floor.

"Ow," Calvin grunted. "Stop hitting me in the *head*!" Pulling his legs up to his chest, he shoved the mayor as hard as he could, sending her flying several yards across the room.

Mayor Balboa caught her balance against a deck chair, snarling at him. Tossing her hair out of the way, she flew forward again, attempting to crush Calvin's windpipe with her foot.

The alien had reached the edge of the pool, leaving a trail of goo smeared on the tile behind it. Reaching out, it dipped a single tentacle over the side, testing the water.

Margot's eyes fell on the vacuum cleaner sitting unattended in front of the pool area's supply closet. With a final, determined slice of the knife, she cut her feet free and stood up.

"What are you doing?" Mateo asked. "Cut me free!"

Margot rolled her head from side to side, planting her feet as she faced Coach Jenkins. "Don't worry," she called. "I've got a plan."

Mateo moaned, closing his eyes.

The alien lowered itself into the pool with a loud splash.

Coach Jenkins continued to advance. He was, of course, grossly underestimating Margot's ability to stop him.

Luckily for the fate of the world, Margot didn't underestimate herself.

Waiting until Coach Jenkins was barely a few feet away, she shot out with a lightning-quick outside penetration step, sweeping his legs beneath him.

Coach Jenkins thudded to the floor in confusion.

The familiar exhilaration of taking down an opponent flooded through Margot's veins. In that moment, she suddenly remembered everything she loved about wrestling. She took off at a run, her sneaker-clad feet sliding across the goo-smeared floor.

Coach Jenkins heaved himself to his feet, rubbing the back of his head. He hesitated for a second, debating if he should follow Margot, then turned to Mateo instead.

Mateo, who had opened one eye to watch Margot, promptly squeezed both of them shut again.

A few yards away, Calvin and Mayor Balboa continued to grapple with each other, panting loudly with exertion.

Margot's shoes squeaked against the tile as she rounded the corner of the pool. With an angry growl, Chelsea rounded the corner from the other side. She crashed into Margot, attempting to knock her into the water.

Margot wasn't proud of what she did next.

Grabbing Chelsea around the waist, she lifted the smaller girl up, executed a one-hundred-and-eighty-degree turn, and flung her into the pool. Chelsea back-flopped into the water with a loud shriek of anger.

The spinebuster, as this particular move was known, was very popular with professional television wrestlers throughout the world. It was, as her father had often reminded her, nothing more than a cheap, amateurish trick.

It was also very effective.

As Chelsea spluttered to the surface, kicking angrily, Margot lunged toward the vacuum cleaner.

Coach Jenkins paused in front of Mateo. "Sorry 'bout this, son," he grunted, raising a meaty fist in the air. "Nothing personal."

Mateo squeezed his eyes shut tighter, waiting.

There was a whoosh of air, and then a thud, and then nothing.

Mateo cautiously cracked his eye open again.

His dad stood in front of him, holding the pool skimmer. The aluminum frame was bent where it had connected with the side of Coach Jenkins's head.

He looked down at Mateo in confusion, wavering slightly on his feet.

"Did I just do that?" he asked.

Mateo smiled up at him. "Yep," he said. "I'm pretty sure you did."

Mayor Balboa drew back, preparing to slam Calvin's head into the ground for what looked like it might be the final time.

On the other side of the pool, Margot jammed her foot down on the pedal of the vacuum cleaner. Everyone in the room turned to look as it roared to life.

Chelsea's eyes widened in realization. Shrieking, she hauled herself out of the water to safety.

Margot picked the vacuum up, her muscles straining as she lifted it over her head.

With a loud, triumphant cry, she tossed the still-whirring machine into the pool.

The electrical current running through the vacuum spread instantly through the water. It reacted poorly with the bioluminescent space goo coating the alien creature.

To make a long and exceedingly technical description short, the Alien Queen exploded.

Pieces of it flew everywhere, splattering the surrounding walls and deck chairs with goo. Globs of bluish alien meat fell through the air like hail, and a large piece of tentacle landed on Margot's head.

The smell of fried alien was almost as bad as the stench of the decaying whale outside.

Mayor Balboa stopped mid-punch, confusion flooding her face.

The tentacle piece slid wetly down Margot's cheek, splatting quietly to the ground. Silence fell over the room.

Mateo's dad let his pool skimmer fall from his hand. Tottering unsteadily on his feet, he reached back and pulled the now unmoving alien away from his neck. It came free easily with a soft sucking noise.

"Huh," he said weakly. "Look at that."

Overhead, a skylight shattered.

A dozen black-clad commandos rappelled into the pool area.

Chelsea raised her head, water dripping from her chin onto the floor. "Just so you know," she told the commandos. "*None* of this was my fault."

CHAPTER 33

THE UNITED STATES ARMY WAS nothing if not organized.

Within half an hour, the Cozy Inn's pool area had been cleared of possible extraterrestrial threats and roped off from the public. Medical professionals had been called in to treat the infected townspeople, while army scientists had begun to prepare the remaining viable alien tissue samples for transport.

Even the glass from the shattered skylight had been swept up and disposed of properly.

Margot couldn't help being impressed by the efficiency of it all. She was less impressed with the way the army official in front of her was treating her like a child.

"So you honestly expect us to believe that you're

Rolly Valverde," Margot said, running her eyes up and down the man in front of her. "From the alien website."

Sitting next to her in the back of a parked ambulance, Mateo wrinkled his nose skeptically. "No offense, dude, but you don't exactly look like a lifeguard."

Margot nodded, keeping her expression serious. "It's the face," she said. "Too pale. A *real* lifeguard would be tanner."

"And also probably wearing a swimsuit," Mateo added. "Instead of, you know . . ." He gestured vaguely at the heavily armored fatigues the man was wearing. "That."

Special Agent Dyer, as he had introduced himself to Margot and Mateo, gave them an impassive look. "'Rolly Valverde' is a cover alias, as is his website. The United States government uses the site to covertly monitor any contact with alien entities. When you filled out the website's email form, we used your information to lock onto your location and dispatch a tactical team to the area."

Margot and Mateo stared at him.

"Uh, yeah," Mateo said. "We pretty much got that after the first couple of times one of you guys explained it to us."

"It's getting a little old," Margot agreed. "No offense."

A muscle in Agent Dyer's cheek twitched. "We find most people need the repetition. Realizing they've been in contact with an alien life-form tends to be . . . overwhelming. Although I must say," he begrudgingly admitted, "the two of you seem to be taking the news with impressive restraint."

Margot shrugged. "I guess we're not most people," she said.

"Plus, we figured out the whole 'alien' thing hours ago," Mateo said.

"Pretty much right away," Margot agreed. "I mean, it was kind of obvious, when you looked at all of the facts."

Agent Dyer's cheek twitched again.

"Matty," Rodrigo croaked from behind him, pulling his air mask aside. "Stop teasing the poor man. He's just doing his job."

Mateo turned to look at his dad then gave a groan of frustration. "*Dad*," he said, scrambling back toward the ambulance cot his father was lying on. "What are you doing? You're supposed to keep that thing *on*."

As Mateo fussed over his father, Margot turned back to Agent Dyer. "There's something I'm curious about," she said, leaning forward.

"*One* thing?" he asked, arching an eyebrow.

"The boxes," she said. "The ones in the pool area.

Were they planning on shipping something in them? The mayor mentioned 'precious cargo.'"

Agent Dyer gave Margot an appraising look. "You picked up on that, huh?"

"So what was she talking about?" Margot asked. "The mayor?"

The special agent glanced over his shoulder, making sure that no one was listening to their conversation.

"This is in the strictest confidence," he warned.

Margot nodded eagerly.

"I'm only telling you because we've been after this so-called Alien Queen for a long time now. Longer than you've been alive, probably."

Margot gestured impatiently for him to continue with a wave of her hand. "Wait!" She had an epiphany. "It was eggs, right?"

Agent Dyer blinked. "What?"

"*Eggs*," Margot repeated. "It's the only thing that makes sense. You couldn't ship live aliens, because they need a host to survive. You know, with how they suck all the moisture and nutrients and stuff out of people's bodies? But eggs, well . . . it makes sense. I'm right, aren't I?"

Agent Dyer blinked a second time. "Yes," he said finally. "You're right."

Margot grinned in satisfaction, drumming her heels

against the back of the ambulance. "I knew it."

"Although, luckily, no eggs were recovered on-site," he said. "We're hypothesizing that the 'queen,' as she was known, was still in the process of preparing to lay them." He shook his head. "I *really* shouldn't be telling you this."

Margot held her hand up, pretending to zip her lips. "Your secret's safe with me," she promised. "Besides," she said. "You've already made us sign, like, a billion nondisclosure forms."

"Which are to be taken seriously," Agent Dyer warned. "Believe me, the last thing you want is for us to come back here."

"Like anyone would even believe us if we did tell," Mateo said, sitting back down beside Margot. "You guys have already gotten rid of all of the evidence."

Agent Dyer nodded at him. "This isn't our first rodeo, son. Although before we go wheels up, let me congratulate the both of you on your accomplishment today. You're done your country a great service. You've done the *world* a great service." Snapping his legs together, Agent Dyer straightened his shoulders, giving Margot and Mateo a crisp salute. "On behalf of the United States Army, we thank you."

And with that, he turned on his heel and strode quickly away.

Mateo looked at Margot. "Seriously?" he asked. "That's it?" He flipped his sunglasses down on his nose, watching as Agent Dyer walked away.

"I can't believe you still have those," Margot said, squinting at him. "How are they not broken?"

Mateo shuddered. "Don't even joke about that." He reached up, giving the glasses a reassuring pat.

They sat in silence for a moment, watching the bustle of activity around them. Several ambulances had been dispatched from the surrounding towns, and were now ringed around the Cozy Inn's parking lot in a loose semicircle.

Almost all the previously infected adults were being treated for some level of dehydration, though only a few cases were as bad as Mateo's father.

The West Cove newspaper reporters had arrived, although army officials had cordoned them off away from the parking lot. Mayor Balboa, who was weak but still upright, was giving a short press conference about the "localized gas leak" and "consequent minor explosion" that had occurred earlier at the Cozy Inn.

A paramedic stood impatiently off to the side, waiting for her to finish so that he could hook up her IV.

"Weird day, huh?" Mateo asked.

Margot couldn't help grinning. "It was definitely interesting, at least."

"And the vacuum just made the alien . . . explode?" Mateo asked.

The actual explanation for why the alien exploded involved phrases like "liquid viscosity" and "fluid dynamic heat transfer." Margot had overheard one of the army commandos explaining the process to Calvin, who was practically grinning in glee as he nodded along.

"Yep," Margot said. "Pretty much."

"Weird," Mateo said again, shaking his head.

Margot sighed. "I can't believe we discovered an *alien life-form* and we're not even going to get recognized for it," she said wistfully. "It would have been the most important discovery of the century. We would have been in every scientific journal in the world. I bet we could have even toured NASA, if we wanted."

"And, you know, we probably would have been, like, rich and famous," Mateo added. "That part would have been nice, too."

Margot rolled her eyes.

Clutching a tinfoil blanket around her shoulders, Chelsea made her way up to the back of Margot and Mateo's ambulance. Her still-wet hair hung limply down her back, and her eyeliner was smeared across her cheeks.

"Hey," she said, pulling the blanket more tightly

around herself. She offered Margot and Mateo a hesitant smile. "These army guys are pretty intense, huh?"

Margot shrugged. "A little."

Mateo pushed his sunglasses up, looking down at Chelsea with a glare. "FYI, my Xbox is totally broken, by the way," he said. "You couldn't have picked something else to smash over Calvin's head?"

Chelsea flinched. "Sorry," she said guiltily. "It was, like, *me*, but it wasn't me, you know? Like I was watching a movie of myself or something." She hitched her blanket a little higher on her shoulders. "I hope I didn't hurt him."

"He's fine," Mateo said. "I think that dude's got, like, a Wolverine metal plate in his head or something." He nodded toward Calvin, who was eagerly trotting behind one of the army scientists, his lips moving a mile a minute as he bombarded them with questions. A large white splint had been fastened over Calvin's nose, which the mayor had apparently broken during the fray.

"I'm pretty sure he's having the time of his life," Margot said.

"Still," Chelsea said. "I feel bad. I should write him an apology note or something. Although, technically—"

"None of this is your fault," Margot and Mateo chorused at the same time, finishing Chelsea's sentence.

"Well, it's *not*," Chelsea said defensively. She started to flick her hair behind her shoulder then realized it was wet. "Anyway," she said instead. "We should head back."

"Back where?" Mateo asked.

Chelsea looked at him as though the answer was obvious. "Hello? School? We have the play tonight."

"Seriously?" Mateo asked. "The play's still happening?"

"Why wouldn't it be?" Chelsea asked.

"Um, I don't know." Mateo gestured around the Cozy Inn's lawn. *"Aliens."*

"Localized gas leak," Margot corrected him. "Remember?"

"Hey, I'm just following orders," Chelsea said. "The army guy told me we're supposed to 'return to our normal schedules as soon as possible to avoid arousing suspicion.'"

"The show must go on," Margot quoted. "Besides, the PTA is having a bake sale during intermission."

Mateo snorted. "Right. Because that's what we should be worrying about right now. A *bake sale*." Still, he pushed himself up. "I'm going to go with my dad to the hospital. But I'll meet you at the school, okay?"

"Do you want to ride with me?" Chelsea asked Margot. "My parents are coming to get me. I need to shower, but they can drop you off at home first." She ran her eyes up and down, eyeing Margot critically. "You should probably grab a shower, too," she said. "You're kind of . . . covered in goo."

Margot opened her mouth to tell Chelsea that she'd be fine on her own.

But then she hesitated.

Just because she *was* fine on her own didn't mean she always *had* to be.

Did it?

"Okay," she said, sliding awkwardly off the back of the ambulance. "That'd be . . . good. Thanks."

"No problem," Chelsea said. "Wait here a sec, I'll go see if they're here yet."

Mateo waved from the back of the ambulance, where one of the paramedics was pulling the back doors shut. "See you soon," he called cheerfully to Margot. "Oh, and thanks for saving my life! I owe you one!"

Margot waved, shivering a little in her hoodie as the ambulance pulled away. The sun had ducked behind the clouds, and the wind off the ocean had grown suddenly cold. The adrenaline she'd been running on all day was starting to fade. And now that she was just sitting there, the stench of the decaying whale was worse than ever.

"Margot! I thought you might want these back."

Margot turned to see Calvin jogging up behind her, holding her and Mateo's cell phones in his hand, as well as the keys to Mateo's dad's convertible. His bandaged nose looked extremely painful, and his eyes were dark and swollen from where he had been punched.

Twice.

Still, he was grinning.

"Thanks," Margot said, taking the phones from him. "Are you sure you're feeling okay?" she asked, wincing a little as she peered more closely at his nose.

"Are you kidding me?" Calvin asked. "We just stopped *aliens* from taking over the world. I'm great!" His grin faded a little as the white NOAA van pulled into the parking lot. Dr. Smalls's scowl was clearly visible through the windshield as he surveyed the scene unfolding in front of the Cozy Inn.

He sighed, mentally resigning himself to four hundred and eighty-six more days of fetching sandwiches and scrubbing out specimen jars. "Too bad the army doesn't need another scientist, huh? I'd kill to be involved with the work that's about to happen," he told Margot wistfully, staring at the unmarked boxes of alien samples being carefully loaded onto an army truck. "I guess it's back to the real world, though. Dr. Smalls and I are due back in Seattle tomorrow." He shuddered, staring at the NOAA van. "Last time he made me pack for him. I had to fold his *underwear*."

Margot suppressed a grin. "Well, if you want to sneak out, you can always come to our play tonight instead."

"Your play?"

"*Romeo and Juliet*," Margot said. "Mateo and I are the leads. But I was kidding. You don't have to—"

"*Biggs!*" Dr. Smalls's voice thundered across the parking lot, cutting her off. As Margot and Calvin turned to look, the doctor climbed heavily out of the van, gesturing around the parking lot. "Just what the heck is going on around here?" Dr. Smalls demanded angrily, stomping toward them. "You've got a lot of explaining to do, son. Starting with why there's *salt* all over the back of our *very expensive* van!"

Calvin turned back to Margot. "What time did you say the play started?"

CHAPTER 34

THE BACKSTAGE AREA AT WEST Cove Middle School was humming with the sort of electric energy that always seems to appear before a performance. Half-costumed students tore through the wings, shrieking with laughter. Black-shirted crew members rushed around, making last-minute adjustments to the scenery.

Margot sat in one of the dressing rooms, staring curiously into a mirror.

A stranger stared back at her.

Her thick, unruly, blue-streaked hair was hidden beneath a wig of long, glossy ringlets that fell perfectly to her waist. She was wearing a dark green velvet gown instead of her usual jeans and hoodie, and velvet slippers instead of sneakers. Her lips were pink, her cheeks were red, and her eyes were rimmed in black.

"What do you think?" Chelsea asked. She pursed her lips, looking critically at Margot's face. "More eyeliner?"

"Um, I'm not sure," Margot said. "What do *you* think?"

Chelsea gave a nod. "Definitely more. Close your eyes."

Margot obediently tilted back her head as Chelsea leaned forward, flicking back her nurse's wimple. She tried not to flinch as Chelsea began to trace another thick layer of eye pencil above her lashes.

"I don't really wear makeup, usually," Margot admitted. "It feels a little weird."

"Try not to talk," Chelsea instructed her. "It makes your eyelids move."

"Oh. Sorry. I mean, whoops. Sorry." Margot shut her mouth tightly, beginning to sweat beneath her velvet gown.

The fact that Chelsea Mandetti was applying her makeup seemed almost as bizarre as aliens invading West Cove.

"You look really good," Chelsea said, starting on the other eye. "Seriously. Like, I can barely recognize you."

Margot was confused. Was Chelsea saying that she

looked good? Did she mean she usually looked *bad*?

She was happy that she had an excuse not to open her mouth.

Chelsea traced another thick line of pencil around Margot's eye. Margot winced a little at the pressure.

"There," Chelsea said, leaning back. "Perfect."

Margot opened her eyes, turning to look at the dressing table mirror again. "Wow," she said. "That's . . . a lot of eyeliner."

"I know, right?" Chelsea said. She capped the eyeliner, tossing it onto the dressing table. She peered into the mirror next to Margot, straightening the wimple of her nurse's costume. "I'm just glad my dad let me back out of the house after the whole 'gas leak' thing," she said, using her fingers like quotation marks. "Honestly, for a second there I thought he was going to tie me to my bed and force chicken noodle soup down my throat."

Margot gave a fake groan, pretending to sympathize.

She'd talked to her mom, of course, who was already in the car, speeding home from her meeting in Olympia as quickly as she could. But her cat, Stampy, had been the only one there to greet her when Chelsea's parents had dropped her off at her house.

After she finished the phone call with her mother, Margot had thought about calling her dad, her fingers hesitating over the screen of her phone.

In the end, though, she'd hadn't done it.

After all, she told herself, her dad knew her number.

This time, he could be the first one to call.

Chelsea smoothed her eyebrow with her finger. "So are you coming out tonight?" she asked. "After the play? A bunch of us are going to the diner."

"Oh." Margot stared at her reflection in the mirror again. "Maybe?" she asked nervously. "I don't know. Is Mateo going?"

Chelsea gave her eyebrow a final pat, turning to look at Margot. "Yeah. Everyone is." She wrinkled her forehead. "You don't, like, *like* him, do you?"

"What?" Margot asked. "No! We're just . . . friends."

"Okay," Chelsea said. "Good. That's good." She turned back to the mirror, straightening her costume one final time. "I'm going to go grab a drink. Break a leg, or whatever."

"You, too," Margot said distractedly. On the dressing table in front of her, Mateo's cell was vibrating. "Oh, hey," she called after Chelsea, picking up the phone. "Can you give this to Mateo if you . . ."

Her words died in her throat at the sight of the text illuminated on the screen.

It was from Todd Morgan.

It read: "have fun kissing Large-O 2nite, sucker"

CHAPTER 35

THE SHOW, AS THE SAYING goes, went on.

Margot's performance was flawless; she sighed when she was supposed to sigh, she smiled when smiles were called for, she gazed lovingly at Mateo when gazing lovingly at Mateo was required. . . . Once, she even managed a few real tears by pinching herself on the arm.

As far as the audience was concerned, Margot made a perfect Juliet.

But looks can be deceiving.

On the inside, Margot felt nothing like the character she was playing. She felt ugly. She felt stupid. For the first time in her life, she felt small.

A tiny part of her kept whispering that she should

have known. She should have realized that Mateo wasn't really her friend. That behind her back, he'd been mocking her every time she sat down next to him, or talked to him, or made the mistake of looking in his direction.

The whole time, he had been laughing at her.

Everyone had been laughing at her.

She dug her fingernails into her palms.

"But my true love is grown to such excess," she told Mateo, smiling up at him. "I cannot sum up sum of half my wealth."

"Come, come with me, and we will make short work," boomed Alex Jeffreys, who was playing the role of the friar. "For, by your leaves, you shall not stay alone till Holy Church incorporate two in one."

Clasping Mateo's hand, Margot hurried offstage with Mateo and Alex to the sound of thunderous applause from the audience.

As soon as they reached the wings, she snatched her fingers away, crossing her arms across her chest. Mrs. Fournier, the director, announced the play's intermission over the loudspeaker.

"I'm, like, drowning in sweat here," Alex said, tugging uncomfortably at his friar's robes. "How come you get to wear pants?" he asked Mateo.

Mateo looked down at his velvet-encased legs. "I think they're technically tights," he said.

"I'm going to go get something to drink," Margot mumbled, turning away.

"I'll come with you," Mateo said, starting to fall into step beside her. "Hey, did Chelsea mention the diner later? I'm just going for a minute, so I can get a burger and smuggle it into the hospital for my dad, but you should come. It'll be fun."

Something inside Margot snapped.

"No, I'm not going to the diner, okay? Just leave me *alone*."

"What?" Mateo literally fell back a step, confusion flooding his face. "Are you okay? Did I say something?"

"You didn't need to," Margot said, reaching into the inner pocket of her velvet costume. "I *read* it."

"Read *what*?" Mateo asked. "I have no idea what you're talking about!"

As crew members in black T-shirts hurried around them, preparing the set for Act III, Margot handed Mateo back his phone. "I saw Todd's text, okay? I know you've been laughing at me behind my back. I *know* it." She reached up automatically to tug on her ponytail then realized she was still wearing her wig. "So just . . . stop pretending we're friends, okay? Just stop it."

"I don't know what you're talking about," Mateo said. "*What* text? And we *are* friends. Or at least I thought we were."

Margot felt hysterical laughter welling up in her throat. She pushed it away.

"I know what you all call me behind my back, okay?" she said. "Large-O? I *know* it."

Mateo's hands dropped.

He opened his mouth to defend himself then closed it again.

Margot felt hot tears of shame pricking at the back of her eyelids. She blinked them determinedly away. "From now on, just leave me alone, Mateo. All right? Just leave. Me. *Alone.*"

She whirled away from him, almost knocking over the false stone wall that a crew member had just rolled into place.

Dodging behind the slab of gray-painted foam, she hurried through the wings and past the dressing rooms, heading for the exit. Yanking open the door, Margot slipped outside into the twilight.

She leaned against the brick wall, taking as deep of breaths as her too-tight velvet gown and the disgusting stench of dead whale would allow her.

For a moment, she considered crying.

Determinedly sniffing back tears, she pulled out her own phone, turning it on to check for messages.

There were three missed calls from her mother.

CHAPTER 36

"MOM?" MARGOT ASKED. SHE STRAIGHTENED up, quickly wiping her eyes. Her fingers came away black from Chelsea's eyeliner. "What's up? Are you here?"

"Margot! Not yet, honey. The Twelve is completely backed up. Are you still doing okay?"

Margot cleared her throat. "Mom, I'm fine. I told you, I wasn't anywhere near the gas leak. You're not talking while you're driving, are you?" she asked.

"You're on speaker," Sarah Blumenthal said. "I'm so sorry I'm not there yet. Is it going amazing? What have I missed?"

Visions of gooey alien chunks raining down on her flashed through Margot's head. "Not much," she told her mom. "You know. A couple of sword fights. I didn't fall off the balcony or anything, so that's good."

"Are you sure it's going okay?" Sarah asked. "You sound a little . . . sad."

Margot blinked back another round of tears. She wished her mom were there right now, wrapping her arms around her in a big, vanilla-scented hug. "I'm just really into character," Margot lied. "It's called Method acting."

"All right. Well, I'll be there as soon as I can," Sarah promised. "Sooner, if I don't stop for traffic lights. Knock 'em dead, okay?"

"Okay," Margot said.

"I'm so proud of you, honey. I'll see you afterward!"

Margot hung up, shivering a little as a particularly strong gust of wind swept in from the ocean. From the side parking lot, she could see all the way down to the beach, where the giant bulk of the whale was beached.

She covered her nose with her hand, squinting down at the whale. In the dim glow of the parking lot's lights, she could just make out the yellow crime scene tape surrounding it. It was the same tape that the police always used on television shows.

There was something a little bit sad about the giant creature, just lying there in the darkness.

A lot of people didn't realize it, but whales were some

of the most intelligent creatures on earth. They traveled in close-knit groups, and were fiercely loyal to one another. They even mourned when a member of their pod died.

Margot wondered if anyone was mourning this particular whale at the moment.

She hoped so.

The door scraped open beside her, causing her to jump. "Margot? Are you out here?" Mateo poked his head out of the exit, looking around. "Oh," he said, catching sight of her. "Um, can I come out?"

Margot gave a little shrug. "It's a free country."

"Thanks to us, am I right?" Mateo asked. Margot just looked at him. "Because of how we stopped the aliens?" Mateo stepped outside and leaned against the open door. He gave a little shiver as another gust of wind blew across the parking lot. "You know, when we saved the world, or whatever?"

Margot shrugged again.

"Listen." Mateo hesitated, adjusting the collar of his velvet jacket. "Um, so yeah. I'm sorry about the whole nickname thing," he said quickly, not quite looking at Margot. "It wasn't supposed to be . . . I mean, you were never supposed to . . . It wasn't a big deal," he ended, staring at her forehead. "Honest. It was just . . . a joke."

"Okay," Margot said coolly, her eyes focused on the place where Mateo's dark hair curled around the top of his ear.

"Nobody even thought you'd care, you know? You've barely talked to anyone since you moved here." He shifted uncomfortably, tugging at his tights. "Until today, I mean. But it seemed like you thought you were too good for all of us or something."

Margot's eyes flickered briefly to meet his. "So it's my fault?" she asked. "That's what you're saying?"

Mateo took a step back, shaking his head. "No. I mean, of course not. I shouldn't have . . . It was . . . I'm really sorry. I was just trying to . . . explain."

"Okay," Margot said. "Got it. Thanks."

Mateo hesitated. "Really?"

"Uh-huh," Margot said, staring at his ear again. "I get it."

"Okay," Mateo said hesitantly. "Awesome. So, um . . . still friends?"

Through the open door, Mrs. Fournier's voice echoed loudly from the wings: "All cast and crew to the stage, please! All cast and crew to the stage!"

Margot pushed off from the wall.

Her anger had suddenly faded. She just felt exhausted.

As Mateo hesitated in the doorway, she gave a little

tug on the side of her wig, smoothing it over her fore-head. "It's fine," she said. "Let's just . . . talk about it later. Or not."

Mateo hesitated for a second then nodded. "Okay. I really am sorry, you know."

Margot nodded.

She believed him.

She just wasn't sure if it was enough.

"Cast and crew to the stage!" Mrs. Fournier called again, in a slightly manic voice. "Where are our leads, people?"

"Come on," Margot said. "Let's go in before Mrs. Fournier has a heart attack."

Mateo held the door open for Margot, gesturing for her to go first.

As Margot slipped back into the school, she glanced out at the huge, shadowy figure of the beached whale.

For a second, she could swear she saw something glowing inside of it.

CHAPTER 37

MRS. FOURNIER WAS RUSHING ABOUT frantically, moving props to their correct places and shooing people from the stage. "Margot, Mateo, there you are!" she whispered, catching sight of them as they appeared from the wings. "Where have you been? Never mind! Mateo, do you have your weapon?"

Mateo wordlessly held up his prop sword.

Mrs. Fournier beamed at him. "Remember, the action needs to flow naturally. You don't *intend* to murder Tybalt. You're just so overcome from the loss of your beloved friend, Mercutio, that you lose all control."

"Er, yep," Mateo said, sheathing his sword. "You got it."

"*Wonderful* job so far, Margot," Mrs. Fournier said. "Just wonderful. Keep it up. Remember, the strongest emotion is yet to come."

"Uh-huh," Margot said. "Will do." She turned away without looking at Mateo, heading back to the wings to wait for her cue.

There was something tugging at the corner of her brain, but she couldn't quite pin down what it was. The strange glow that she had seen coming from the whale could have just been a trick of the light. A reflection from the parking lot, or the moon glancing off a patch of water.

But then why was it bothering her so much?

And why did she keep feeling like she was missing something?

Margot shook her head in frustration.

She wasn't used to missing things.

As feelings went, it wasn't her favorite.

The second half of the play seemed to fly by almost more quickly than the first. Margot sleepwalked through her performance, barely hearing the applause from the crowd after each scene.

Trying to figure out *what* she was missing only made it slip further away.

Margot was sitting, frustrated, in the wings, right

before the big finale when Chelsea slid into the seat next to hers. "Hey. Mateo told me what happened," she said matter-of-factly. "About the Large-O thing?"

"Oh," Margot said stiffly. "That."

Chelsea made a face. "Todd is such a tool. I don't even know why people hang out with him. He used to pee on the slide in elementary school. Anyway," she said. "My point is that you shouldn't let him bother you. He's like a mosquito or something. Totally annoying, but if you ignore him, he'll just go away." She paused, considering. "Or wait, *do* mosquitoes go away? Or do you have to swat them?" She shook her head. "Either way works, I guess."

"Thanks," Margot said. "But it's not like Todd was the only one calling me"—she cleared her throat—"it's not like Todd was the only one."

Chelsea waved her away. "Please. You got off lucky. When Sarah Rutthead moved here in the fifth grade, it was *rough*." She stood back up, straightening her costume. "Anyway, who cares? Come to the diner tonight. It'll be fun. I promise."

Margot opened her mouth to decline. But at that exact moment, the thing that had been bothering her, the thing that she couldn't *quite* figure out, fell into place.

Into terrifying, mind-numbing place.

She bounced out of her chair, nearly knocking Chelsea over. "I've got to go," she said, gathering her skirt with her hands. "Something just came . . . I mean, I just realized . . ." She shook her head, trying to focus her thoughts. "I think we made a mistake. Or the army guys made a mistake. What if—"

Chelsea held up her hand, cutting her off. "If this is about aliens, I so *don't* want to know."

"Right," Margot said. "Okay. You're right. But I've got to go. Thanks for the . . . thanks." With a final nod, she took off for the wings.

"Good luck saving the world, or whatever!" Chelsea called after her.

With a final flick of her nurse's wimple, she ambled away.

CHAPTER 38

"MATEO," MARGOT HISSED, RUNNING TOWARD the stage. "I need to talk to you!"

"What?" Mateo whispered. He waved from the edge of the stage, where he was waiting in the wings. "I can't hear you."

Margot started toward him, only to have Mrs. Fournier plant herself firmly in front of her. "What do you think you're doing?" the director asked, clicking her tongue in annoyance. She pushed Margot toward the fake stone slab she was supposed to be lying on when the curtain came up. It was the final, famous "death scene" of *Romeo and Juliet* which was, admittedly, not great timing.

"I just need to talk to Mateo. For just a minute," Margot said, trying to slip away.

"*After,*" Mrs. Fournier said firmly. "Hop on," she added, patting the gray construction paper-covered table. "Now!"

Mrs. Fournier ducked back into the wings as the curtain began to rise ahead of the cue. Margot clambered hurriedly onto the table, pretending to lie still.

Mateo burst onto the stage, staggering a little as he propped Dashon Shield's limp body up on his shoulder. Dashon, who was playing the character of Paris and had just been killed in the play, released Mateo's arm and let himself sink to the floor. Still panting, Mateo began his big monologue. The speech was a doozy; at the end of it, Romeo was supposed to die, but not before kissing his true love, Juliet, one last time.

On the cheek, of course.

It was, after all, a middle school performance.

"O, what more favor can I do to thee, than with that hand that cut thy youth in twain," Mateo said dramatically, peering down at Margot.

"Mateo," Margot whispered, trying to keep her lips from moving. "I just realized something."

Mateo blinked, momentarily forgetting his lines.

"Er, eyes, look your last," he said, gesturing distractedly with his sword. "Arms, take your last embrace."

"Mateo," Margot hissed, cracking an eye open. "The mayor. At the hotel, she was talking about 'precious cargo,' remember?"

"So?" Mateo whispered. "Um, come, bitter conduct!" Mateo said in a louder voice, half-turning toward the audience. "Come, unsavory guide!"

"So she meant *eggs*," Margot whispered. "They were planning on shipping alien eggs. Only Agent Dyer said the Alien Queen hadn't laid them yet."

"Okay. But that's a good thing, isn't it?" Mateo shook his head, turning back to the audience. "Here's to my love!" he practically boomed. Pulling a small vial from his pouch, he crouched down next to Margot and pretended to drink the "poison" inside.

Margot turned to him, forgetting that she was supposed to be playing dead. "I think he's wrong," she said. "The Alien Queen *did* lay eggs. And I think I know where."

Mateo stared, horrified, down at her. "What?"

"The *whale*," Margot said. "Your dad was the first one to find it, right? And the Queen didn't get to the hotel by herself."

Realization dawned across Mateo's face. "His conservation group," he said. "They were all the sickest.

They must have been infected first."

Margot sat up, her fake, golden curls tumbling down her back. "This could be bad, Mateo. *Really* bad. We have to at least check!"

He looked dubiously over his shoulder. A quiet buzz was building in the audience as they began to shift in their seats, wondering what the holdup was.

He could see Mrs. Fournier waving frantically at Margot from the wings, gesturing for her to lie down again.

"Fine," he said. "We'll check, okay?"

Margot nodded. Pulling off her wig, she tossed it to the floor.

Someone in the audience actually gasped in surprise.

"What, right now?" Mateo gaped at her. "Shouldn't we die first?"

Margot swung her legs over the side of the table and stood up. "Nope," she said. "Not this time."

CHAPTER 39

MARGOT AND MATEO FLED THROUGH the wings, slipping easily away from their stunned cast mates. "Sorry," Margot called out to Mrs. Fournier as they rushed past the director. "Change of plans! But don't wait for us!"

As they headed for the side door, Margot caught a brief glimpse of Chelsea giving them an encouraging thumbs-up.

Bursting into the parking lot, they dodged through the rows of cars and made their way toward the beach.

Even though it didn't seem possible, the whale somehow managed to smell worse the closer they got.

"I'm going to puke," Mateo groaned, covering his nose with his sleeve. "Seriously. For real this time." He gagged a little, spitting over the edge of the low retaining wall that ran along the side of the parking lot.

Margot felt automatically for her mask, forgetting that she was still in her Juliet costume. The wind whipped her hair angrily around her face, making her shiver in her thin velvet gown. "Careful," she said. "It's rocky down there."

Hitching up her costume, she stuck one leg over the retaining wall then pulled herself over. Mateo followed, and they picked their way slowly down the steep slope toward the beach.

"We should have brought a flashlight," Mateo said, stumbling over a loose stone and pitching forward a few feet.

"It wasn't exactly the world's most thought-out plan," Margot admitted.

"Still, it was kind of awesome how we just left, right?" Mateo asked. "Just, like, out of nowhere?"

Margot rolled her eyes, ducking under the police tape. Standing in front of the whale for the first time, it seemed almost too big to be real: a great, hulking beast that rose like a mountain of graying flesh in front of them.

Mateo gagged again. "I should *not* have eaten so much pizza before the show," he said, staring up at the dead whale. "So, like, what are we supposed to do, now that we're here?"

Margot straightened her shoulders. "If the Alien Queen actually did lay eggs in this thing, there's only one way to find out," she said.

"Um, please tell me we're not going to climb . . . *onto* . . . that thing?" he asked, looking at Margot.

She grinned, hitching up her skirt. "I thought you were a rock climber."

Steeling herself, she placed one velvet-slipper-clad foot onto the surface of the whale, gripping the flipper overhead. The flesh gave slightly under the pressure, but held firm enough to take her weight.

Mateo watched in awe as she took another step, pulling herself off the ground entirely.

"What's it feel like?" he asked.

"Come up here and find out," Margot replied, pulling herself forward to make room.

Mateo took a deep breath then immediately regretted it. Swallowing hard, he placed his foot on the whale, following in Margot's path.

"Do you think it's going to hold us both?" Mateo called, panicking slightly as his shoe sank into the whale's leathery skin. "I mean, is it going to, like, burst or something?"

Margot, who was busy pulling herself upward toward the top of the whale, didn't answer. Mateo grimaced.

"I'm going to take that as a maybe," he said, hoisting himself up after her. He was surprised to discover that scaling the side of the whale *was* a bit like climbing the wall at the West Cove Recreational Center.

Only about a thousand more times disgusting.

And without safety ropes.

Margot paused midway up the whale, panting slightly. She turned to look at Mateo. "This is a lot grosser than I thought it would be," she admitted.

"Hey, it was your idea," Mateo said.

"Don't remind me," Margot muttered. She winced as a pocket of gas shifted beneath the whale's skin, releasing a belch of fresh methane.

"Sick!" Mateo shouted, nearly losing his grip. "For the record, *I hate this.*"

"I'm not exactly having fun here, either," Margot snapped. The two of them struggled on, hauling themselves hand over hand to the top of the whale. The shifting gas-filled surface made it difficult.

"Whoa," Mateo said, holding his hands out for balance and peering over the side of the whale. "We're, like, pretty high up right now."

Margot, who was secretly a little nervous around heights, kept her eyes firmly on the back of the whale.

Mateo bounced cautiously up and down on the soles of his feet a few times. "It's kind of like a trampoline," he observed.

"You realize this thing's skin could burst, and you could fall inside, right?" Margot asked.

Mateo stopped bouncing.

"So, uh, what's the plan?" he asked. "I mean, I don't see any eggs just lying around, or anything. If they really are in here, how are we supposed to find them?"

Margot pursed her lips, staring at the sword fastened around Mateo's waist. "I don't know," she said. "Can you cut with that thing?"

Mateo looked down at the scabbard he still wore around his waist. "No," he said quickly, unable to keep the relief from his voice. "It's foam."

Margot looked momentarily stumped.

And then it hit her. "The blowhole," she said eagerly.

"The what?" Mateo asked.

"The blowhole! You know, the waterspout thingy? It should be up here somewhere." She crawled carefully forward, her knees sinking awkwardly into the whale as she moved back and forth, searching.

"Here," she called a few seconds later. "I forgot they were on the left side in sperm whales."

Mateo, who had never known this information to begin with, edged slowly up to meet Margot. The blowhole was encased in what appeared to be a giant pair of lips, sticking out of the side of the whale's head.

"Gross," Mateo observed.

Margot shrugged in silent agreement.

A whale's blowhole is not the most attractive thing in the world.

"Okay," she said. "So now we just have to . . . verify . . . that the eggs are in there."

Mateo looked down at the blowhole. "Really?" he asked. "Are you sure?"

"There's only one way to find out," Margot said, giving him a bright smile. "Paper, Scissors, Rock?"

CHAPTER 40

"WHO SAYS, 'PAPER, SCISSORS, ROCK,' anyway?" Mateo grumbled, tugging off his velvet jacket and tossing it to the side.

The plain white T-shirt he wore underneath looked slightly odd with his blue velvet tights.

"Everyone knows it's 'Rock, Scissors, Paper,'" he told Margot accusingly, crawling toward the blowhole.

Margot shrugged.

"We can do two out of three, if you want," she offered.

Mateo looked tempted for a moment.

He peered down at the blowhole, attempting to see inside. "This is going to be bad, isn't it?"

"Probably."

He sighed. "All right. Let's just get it over with."

Margot gave him an encouraging smile.

Mateo squeezed his eyes shut. "One," he counted to himself. "Two."

And, before he reached three, he plunged his arm quickly into the blowhole. He gasped, his eyes popping open.

"Is it bad?" Margot asked interestedly. "What does it feel like?"

Mateo gritted his teeth. "Not. Good." The inside of the decaying whale's blowhole felt exactly as though he had just thrust his arm inside a trash bag full of warm, rotten steak.

It other words, it felt *not good at all.*

Leaning forward a little more, Mateo thrust his arm deeper into the hole, feeling around inside.

Margot leaned forward as well. "Is anything in there?"

"Give me a minute," he grunted, straining with his arm. At last, his hand closed around something roundish.

It was slightly too large for him to lift.

Groaning, he thrust his other arm into the blowhole, lying his head flat against the whale's surface as he scrabbled around inside.

After what felt like an eternity to Mateo, he pulled his hands free.

A single, pulsating egg the size of a snow globe was cradled in his hands, its translucent skin glowing blue against the darkness.

Margot inhaled quickly.

The egg was full of minuscule, eel-like creatures, thousands upon thousands of them writhing and tangling with one another inside the sac.

"It's swarming with them," Margot said in awe.

"Yeah." Mateo gave an involuntary shiver, almost dropping the egg. "What should I do with it?" he asked.

Margot debated for a moment.

"I have no id—"

"Hello? Margot? Mateo? Are you guys up there?"

Mateo and Margot looked at each other. Crawling forward, they peered cautiously over the side of the whale at the beach below them. The beam of a high-powered flashlight almost blinded them. "Calvin?" Margot asked, shielding her eyes. "What are you doing down there?"

"I was worried when you ran off so I came looking for you," Calvin said. "Sound carries off the ocean, you know. What are you guys doing up there, anyway?"

Mateo held the glowing egg aloft for Calvin to see.

"The Alien Queen laid eggs," he said. "Margot figured it out."

Calvin stared at the egg. Then he stared at the whale. Then he stared at the egg again.

He opened his mouth.

Then he closed it.

He stared at the egg again.

"Do you think you could maybe skip ahead to the part where you're actually helpful?" Margot called down at him. "Because these suckers could hatch any minute."

CHAPTER 41

MATEO ALMOST LOST HIS HOLD on the egg. "Hatch? What? They're going to *hatch*?" He held the pulsating egg a little farther away from his body, looking worried.

"Of course they're going to hatch," Margot said. "What did you think eggs did?"

"I *don't* think about eggs!" Mateo said. "I just *eat* them!"

"How many of them are there?" Calvin called back, finding his voice.

Margot looked at Mateo. "I don't know." He shrugged. "I could only reach this one."

"Toss me your flashlight," Margot called down to Calvin.

He obediently threw the light up, where Margot caught it neatly in one hand. Shimmying back to the blowhole, she aimed the flashlight inside.

There was a long beat.

"Uh-oh," she said.

"What?" Calvin yelled. "What did she say?"

Mateo stuck his head over the side of the whale again. "She said, 'uh-oh,'" he told Calvin.

"Oh," Calvin said. He scratched at his chin. "Well, that can't be good."

Margot joined Mateo at the edge of the whale. "Yeah. I don't think a vacuum cleaner's going to cut it this time," she said.

"Plus, where would we even plug it in?" Mateo asked, looking around at the beach.

"We need to contact the army," Margot said. "They'll know what to do. I mean, this is literally what they've been training for."

"Forget the army," Mateo said. "Do you know how much TMZ would pay for this thing?" He nodded toward the egg. "We'd be rich. Like, NFL rich."

"You know the army isn't going to allow anyone access to their findings," Calvin argued. "When you think about it, denying the world such an important discovery is actually really irresponsible. I mean, who knows what scientists could do with it? For all we know, alien DNA could cure every disease in the world."

The three of them stared at the luminous egg cradled in Mateo's hands. The unborn aliens writhed slowly inside, twisting and wriggling against one another.

There was a long pause.

"Or maybe we should just blow them up," Margot said.

Mateo nodded. "That's probably a good idea. I mean, have you seen a single movie about aliens? Keeping one alive to, like, study it, or whatever, is *never* a good idea."

Calvin reached up to tug thoughtfully at a lock of hair. "How many of them did you say there are?" he asked.

"A lot," Margot said, sitting back on her heels. "A *lot.*"

Calvin made a decision.

"Okay," he called up. "Hold on a second!"

Margot and Mateo watched in interest as he jogged away from the whale, scaling the rocky incline toward the parking lot.

"Where do you think he's going?" Mateo asked.

"I don't know," Margot said. "I don't *think* he's running away, do you?"

Mateo shrugged. "Do you think I can put this back?" he asked, looking down at the glowing alien egg in his hand. "It's starting to weird me out."

It was Margot's turn to shrug. "I'm not the boss of you."

"Right. Okay." Mateo inched forward a few feet then stopped. "Hey, are you sure we're cool? Becau—"

"I don't want to talk about it right now," Margot said, cutting him off. "Let's just . . . wait for Calvin, okay?"

"Okay," Mateo said. "It's just that—"

"Quietly," Margot added. "Let's just wait here quietly."

Mateo nodded. "Yeah. You just seem—"

"*Mateo*," Margot said. "Just *stop talking*."

Mateo stopped talking. The two of them waited in silence until Calvin reappeared on the beach, clutching a large scuba-diving tank in his arms.

He grinned at Margot and Mateo. "Did somebody order a bomb?"

CHAPTER 42

"ARE WE SURE THIS IS a good plan?" Margot asked, tilting her head back to peer up at the whale. "It seems like it isn't going to work."

Calvin popped his head over the side of the whale. "Of course it's going to work," he said, insulted. "This is pure oxygen. It's only used for decompression dives. It's *highly* reactive. You need special training to handle it."

He disappeared back over the side.

Mateo looked at Margot, raising his eyebrows. "I guess that's a yes?"

"And the flare gun comes in . . . how, exactly?" Margot asked.

"Well, the tank isn't just going to explode on its own," Calvin called. "It needs a catalyst."

"So you're going to put a tank of pure oxygen into a whale's blowhole, and then shoot a tank of pure oxygen with a flare gun," Margot clarified. "While standing on top of the whale."

Calvin's head appeared over the side again. "Do you have a better idea?" he asked.

"I think it's going to be cool," Mateo said. "Do you want me to record it on my phone?"

Calvin paused, considering.

"*No*," Margot said, giving Calvin a look. "He *doesn't*."

Calvin looked momentarily disappointed. "Anyway, it should be fine," he told Margot and Mateo. "Detonating the tank in an enclosed space will contain the blast. I probably won't even feel it from where I'm standing."

"If you say so," Margot said dubiously.

"Ready?" Calvin asked. He gave Margot and Mateo a manic grin, climbing to his feet. He checked the flare gun to make sure it was loaded then gave a satisfied nod.

"This is going to be epic," Mateo breathed, staring up at the whale.

Margot closed her eyes. "Let's just do this," she said. "They must have finished the play; people are starting to leave."

"One," Calvin counted, carefully aiming the flare gun. "Two."

The flare ripped a bright red trail through the darkness, trailing sparks as it disappeared into the blowhole.

Margot flinched, waiting for the explosion.

And waiting.

And waiting.

"Did I miss it?" Mateo asked. "Did it not—"

The blast knocked him and Margot ten feet back, where they thudded to the ground in a (thankfully) sandy patch of beach.

Calvin, meanwhile, was flung into the air as the whale he was standing on exploded with thunderous force. A torrential downpour of dead whale fell from the sky, showering a hundred-yard radius with chunks of decomposing blubber.

By some miracle, Calvin was thrown free of the blast. He came down hard, crashing into the hood of a 2004 Kia Sedona with a loud grunt.

It was exactly as painful as it looked.

Margot pulled herself up into a sitting position, glancing dazedly around the blubber-strewn beach. She had thought the alien exploding all over the Cozy Inn's pool area had been unpleasant. But that was nothing compared to the detonation of a forty-seven-ton beached sperm whale.

Ignoring the dull ringing noise in her ears, Margot squinted up at the parking lot, searching for Calvin. "Calvin?" she called. "Are you okay?"

Flat on his back on top of the Kia's hood, Calvin waved an arm in acknowledgment. "It worked," he croaked weakly. "I told you it would."

Next to Margot, Mateo staggered to his feet. Weaving slightly, he made his way toward the parking lot to look around. "Sick," he breathed. "The car wash is going to be *packed* tonight."

Drawn by the noise of the explosion, audience members were beginning to push their way through the middle school's main doors, staring around in disbelief.

Margot and Mateo slowly picked their way back up the rocky incline, over to the car Calvin was lying on. Groaning loudly, Calvin pushed himself into a sitting position. There was a dent in the Kia's hood where he had landed.

"Are you sure you're okay?" Margot asked, picking a glob of . . . something . . . from her hair. "That was . . ."

"Epic," Mateo finished for her. "Awesomely *epic*." He held out his hand for Calvin to high-five.

Calvin limply raised his own hand, slapping it against Mateo's. "I'm fine," he said. "Totally fine." He gazed around the parking lot, taking in the extent of the damage. "Although something tells me I might be fired for this."

Margot bit her lip. "Sorry."

Calvin waved her away. "It's fine," he said. "Did you know the FBI hired oceanographers? I'd have a badge, and everything."

Margot patted him gently on the shoulder. "Maybe wait a couple of days before you apply," she said. "You know. Just until you're sure you don't have a concussion."

"And maybe let your face heal a little," Mateo added. "Because, honestly? Right now you look pretty busted, dude."

Calvin gave an unsteady nod. "Solid plan. You two are good kids, you know that?" He let himself fall back on the hood of the car. "I think I might take just take a little nap," he said, closing his eyes. "Wake me up when the police get here."

Mateo looked at Margot. "We'll call him an ambulance," she said.

More and more people were streaming through the doors of the middle school now, milling around in confusion and shock. The buzz of voices was growing louder and louder, cries of disbelief mixed with hysterical laughter.

"I can't believe he blew the entire whale up," Margot

said, shaking her head. "I mean, look at this place."

Mateo grinned. "I know. Awesome, right?"

Margot raised her eyebrows.

She had to admit, it was a *little* bit awesome.

"You should go," she said, pulling out her phone. "Be with your dad. I'll wait with Calvin." Someone inside the school turned on the floodlights, illuminating the parking lot chaos. Margot held up her hand to shield her eyes, squinting against the glare.

"Here," Mateo said, reaching behind his back. He pulled something out from the waistband of his tights, holding it out to Margot. "Take these."

Margot stared down at his hand. "Your sunglasses?" she asked blankly.

"They're not *just* sunglasses," Mateo said. "They're vintage Ferrari aviators. From 1976, to be exact. But, yeah. Take them."

"I can't," Margot said, shaking her head. She pulled her hands behind her back. "I mean, they're . . . I saw the picture. Of your mom? I know how important they are to you. I can't just take them."

"I *want* you to have them," Mateo said, thrusting the glasses at her. "Seriously. Think of them as, like, a welcome gift. Or an apology gift, for, you know, the whole . . . Large-O thing. Or a thank-you gift! For, like, saving my life." He met Margot's gaze, his eyes earnest.

"Please," he said. "Just take them."

A warm sensation flooded through Margot's body.

"Okay," she said hesitantly. "Um, thanks."

Reaching out, she took the sunglasses and slipped them onto her nose, peering around the parking lot. "They're really dark."

Mateo nodded. "Yeah."

"*Really* dark," Margot commented. "How do you even see in these things?"

"You'll get used to it," Mateo said. "It just takes a while."

"Do they have UV protection?" Margot asked.

Mateo tipped his head back in frustration. "They just look cool, okay? I'm making a gesture here. Just take them!"

Margot reached up to adjust the sunglasses. "Sorry," she said. "Thank you. They're . . . great. Really."

"So . . . friends?" Mateo asked, sticking out his hand. "For real?"

Margot nodded, the sunglasses almost slipping off her nose. "Yeah," she said, reaching out to take his hand. She gave it a firm shake. "Friends. As long as you're okay with me beating you when wrestling practice starts."

"You're going out for the West Cove team?" Mateo asked in surprise. "I thought you *quit.*"

Margot shrugged. "I don't know. It might be kind of nice to just try wrestling for fun, you know? Maybe even make some more friends?"

Mateo grinned.

There was a small piece of whale blubber stuck in his teeth.

"Yeah," he said. "I do. But you're out of luck when it comes to the whole beating me thing, because *I'm* quitting."

"Really?" she asked. She tilted her head to the side, giving him a considering look. "Why?"

He scuffed his foot against the ground. "I don't know. Maybe you were right about the whole 'me doing stuff just to make other people happy' thing. A *little* bit. Anyway, no offense, but I kind of hate wrestling. Like . . . a lot. Did you know you can get *cauliflower ear* from the mats?"

It was Margot's turn to grin.

"Yeah," she said. "You've got to watch out for cauliflower ear."

"And no more loaning out Xbox games," Mateo said, getting into his stride. "Did you know that's the *third* one of mine that Todd's broken? It's like he's *trying* to do it or something."

"Did he really used to pee down the slide in elementary school?" Margot asked, remembering what Chelsea had told her.

"Yeah," Mateo said, grimacing. "It was a whole thing. We had to have a school assembly, and everything."

Margot wrinkled her nose. "Gross."

"Pretty much," Mateo agreed. His eyes widened as he saw Mrs. Fournier pushing her way determinedly through the crowd, her head swiveling back and forth as if searching for someone. Judging from her grim expression, Mateo had a pretty good idea who she was looking for.

"Er, maybe I won't do any more school plays, either," he said, ducking his head a little to avoid Mrs. Fournier's gaze.

"Margot? *Margot?*"

Margot turned to see her mother pushing her way eagerly through the crowd, her eyes wide with relief.

"Is that your mom? You go," Mateo said. "*I'll* wait with Calvin. But I'll see you at the diner later?"

Margot nodded. "Yeah," she said, smiling. "I'll be there."

With a final wave, she jogged forward to meet her mom, who pulled her close, crushing her in a tight hug.

"What happened?" Sarah Blumenthal asked a minute later, peering around the parking lot over Margot's head. "Are you okay? I'm so sorry, sweetie, I can't believe I missed the whole thing. I got stuck behind this truck carrying a *giant crane*, of all things. Is this part of the play?" she asked dubiously, eyeing the scattered whale pieces. "Some sort of . . . performance art . . . or something?"

"The whale exploded," Margot said. "Probably methane," she said, improvising. "The whale's blubber and skin were containing all of the gaseous buildup."

"Huh," Sarah said. "Weird." She gave Margot a final squeeze then pulled back. "So how was it?" Sarah asked. "The play? Was it amazing?"

"It was good," Margot said. "Really good."

"Tell me everything!" Sarah said. She leaned forward conspiratorially, lowering her voice. "How was the kiss?"

"We settled on a firm handshake," Margot said. "It just seemed like the right choice. Artistically, I mean."

"Oh." Her mom wrinkled her nose. "Well, how did the big death scene go, at least? I'll bet there wasn't a dry eye in the house."

Margot grinned. "Death scenes are overrated," she said, waving cheerfully at Mateo from across the parking lot. "We decided Romeo and Juliet should save the world instead."

ACKNOWLEDGMENTS

Thank you to my amazing editor, Jessica MacLeish, who was incredibly patient and encouraging throughout this entire process. It turns out that second books are hard! My agent, Carrie Hannigan, gives fantastic advice, and I don't know where I'd be without her. Katie Fitch and Aaron Blecha created the world's coolest cover for me, and I'm forever in their debt. Thanks as well to Jessica Berg, Alana Whitman, Mitchell Thorpe, Erin Wallace, and everyone else at Harper-Collins who turned *Margot and Mateo* into an actual book. Charlie Whitney helped me out by reading the final draft, and my son, Wyle, had the all-important task of naming Margot's cat. (Don't worry, Fitz; you can name the next one.) Finally, thanks to my husband, Ben, who might literally be the best person on earth. Stay gold, Ponyboy!

ALSO BY
DARCY MILLER

One summer, two friends, and a whole lot of birds.

ROLL

DARCY MILLER

"Readers will cheer on awkward, quirky Ren as he,
like the pigeons, learns to roll with it."
—*Publishers Weekly*

HARPER
An Imprint of HarperCollinsPublishers

www.harpercollinschildrens.c